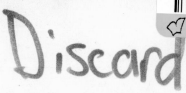

Discard

P9-CEU-545

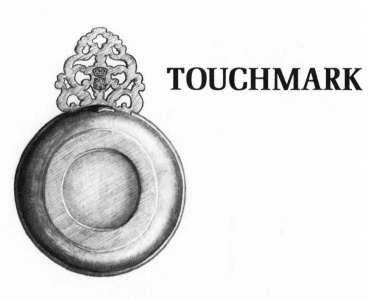

TOUCHMARK

A. J.

TOUCHMARK

by *Mildred Lawrence*

Illustrated by Deanne Hollinger

Harcourt Brace Jovanovich

New York and London

B C D E F G H I J K

Library of Congress Cataloging in Publication Data

Lawrence, Mildred.
Touchmark.

SUMMARY: An orphaned girl living in pre-Revolution-
ary Boston longs to be apprenticed to a pewterer.
1. United States—History—Revolution, 1775–1783—
Juvenile fiction. [1. Orphans—Fiction. 2. United
States—History—Revolution, 1775–1783—Fiction]
I. Hollinger, Deanne. II. Title.
PZ7.L437To   75-11579
ISBN 0-15-289603-1

Opening page art: *porringer*
Title page art: *Nabby's touchmark*
Facing page art: *pewter button mold*

TOUCHMARK

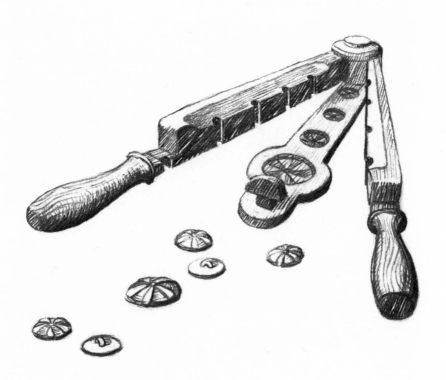

1542

Pewter sky, pewter sea—from her cramped gar-
ret room midway down Long Wharf, Nabby stared
miserably out over Boston Harbor, glossy gray under
gathering storm clouds. Three ships moored just across
the way rocked in the chop. A cluster of peddlers awaiting the arrival of a square-rigger plowing her way past
Castle William, the British island-fortress, stood hud-
dled over a *Gazette* that threatened to blow out of their
hands. Nabby sighed. She dared not even imagine what
it was going to be like to live anywhere except on this
"street that had put out to sea"—Long Wharf that, on
one side, was lined with anchored ships and, on the
other, with a row of warehouses and shops with tiny
living quarters above.

"Abigail Jonas!" A boy's voice sounded shrilly
outside. "Master Pettigrew bids me fetch you posthaste!"

Posthaste, to be looked over like a sheep at the
market! Would it be the mantuamaker who would set
Nabby to stitching hour after hour, year after year, on
fine cloaks for the gentry? Or the wigmaker? Or the
woman who fashioned endless silk and velvet flowers

for ladies' bonnets? All were proper work for a young girl, according to Master Pettigrew, whose task it was to apprentice the poor orphans of Boston in suitable occupations.

Nabby ducked out of sight at the window. Without looking back at the empty room that she might never see again, she picked up the bundle that held her few possessions and crept downstairs to the tiny notions shop, already stripped bare to pay her mother's burial expenses. Here, too, Nabby looked neither to left nor to right but headed straight for the front door and peered cautiously out. The boy who had summoned her was staring openmouthed at a seaman with a gold ring in one ear and a parrot on his shoulder. Nabby slid like an eel behind his back and slipped into the Widow Parsons' tobacco shop next door.

"Pray keep my things for me until later." She thrust her bundle behind the counter. "And if anyone asks, you do not know where I can be found."

"True for you, I do not!" The Widow Parsons, cheerful and round-faced, was passing out a twisted rope of "Virginia pigtail" to a bearded seaman. "And have no fear for your gear. It will be as safe with me as—"

"As in the middle of Boston Harbor," the sailor said with a guffaw.

Safe or not, at least the bundle did not contain Nabby's most treasured possession, the shallow little pewter porringer that her seaman father had brought her from England on his last voyage before he was lost overboard. Nabby had thrust that, marked with a tiny rose and crown impressed on the back, into the deep pocket of her full-skirted linsey-woolsey petticoat so that she might keep it always with her.

"You have heard the news?" the Widow Parsons asked, but Nabby was not interested in news just now. If she missed some today, there would be more tomorrow, for Boston in 1773 was seething with gossip and rumor. With a quick glance outside, Nabby scampered down Long Wharf with her skirts flying and her white cap askew. She almost collided with an old gentleman in a cocked hat at the end of the wharf, where it joined dry land and became cobbled King Street.

"Softly, softly!" He looked at her disapprovingly. "A decorous step and a downcast eye best become a young maid."

"As you say, sir," Nabby said meekly, but her green eyes smoldered as she proceeded at a sober pace until she could dodge down a narrow lane out of the old gentleman's sight. She had already heard quite enough from Master Pettigrew about what best became young maids.

"A pewterer!" he had exclaimed only the day before yesterday, peering at her over the top of his eight-sided spectacles as though he could hardly believe his ears. "You wish to be apprenticed to a pewterer? No, no, my girl! That is suitable only for boys."

"Why?" Nabby had tried to look as large and sturdy as possible—no great effort, since she was tall for fourteen and rather more muscular than some people might consider genteel. "I am strong and much bigger for my age than most boys."

"Quite impossible!" Master Pettigrew had dismissed Nabby's argument out of hand. "Young girls

should not—" Then, as Nabby stared stubbornly at her shoes, "Pray tell me, Abigail Jonas, why you have this improper wish to be apprenticed to a pewterer?"

Nabby tried for the right words.

"I—I would like to learn how to make pewter," she mumbled finally, "because 'tis so—so fair to see."

There was more to it than that, but how could she explain to Master Pettigrew that the muted gray sheen of pewter looked like the harbor on a stormy day? Or that pewter helped keep alive the memory of her father, who had given her the only thing she had ever owned that was bought for beauty, not necessity? She had ended by shaking her head in despair at not being able to make her feelings clear, and Master Pettigrew had said firmly, "A mantuamaker is in need of a likely girl."

Remembering his words, Nabby muttered, "I won't! Never, never, never!" so that a passing British soldier, splendid in scarlet coat and white breeches, said, "What, never?" and swaggered on, laughing. Nabby scowled after him. The Sons of Liberty and a good share of the population of Boston, remembering old grievances, despised the British redcoats as oppressors of the province, even though of late they were garrisoned quietly enough at Castle William. Nabby's frown deepened. The soldier's mocking words reminded her that, for all her talk about "Never, never, never," she would be living at the almshouse tomorrow if she were not apprenticed to some trade today.

Somewhere not far away the town crier was ringing his bell and calling out the news, perhaps announcing the approach of the square-rigger that had been nearing Long Wharf when Nabby left. She hesitated. In case it was the *Boston Traveller,* her father's old ship, it would be only fair to rush back and tell his shipmates that there was no longer any need for them to save the pins, needles, buttons, combs, and battered pewter spoons that they brought in, hidden in their packs, for the Widow Jonas's meager shop. That, Nabby knew, would be good news for the peddlers. She had always beaten them out at the *Boston Traveller*'s arrival, mostly because she was her father's daughter, though partly too because she was not afraid to elbow her way through the crowd of peddlers, eager for anything they could sell in distant villages and farmhouses.

Nabby backtracked to King Street just in time to see the crier going by, but his words, garbled by the wind, seemed to have nothing to do with ships. More than likely it was British taxes, which kept Boston in a perpetual uproar. Nabby had been too occupied of late with her mother's illness and her own problems to fret about such things, although, as she sat by her mother's bedside, angry voices had floated up from the men who frequented the grog shops on Long Wharf.

"Pray steady this broadside while I nail it to yonder tree." A red-haired boy in an apprentice's leathern breeches and vest thrust a flapping sheet of paper into Nabby's hands. "Should it go sailing over Boston like a kite, my master would have me on bread and water for a month."

"And who was your servant last year?" Nabby demanded, but she held the broadside obediently against the tree. Her eyes opened wide. "Why, 'tis Will Truax, twice as well grown as when last I saw you and as full of tales. Bread and water indeed!"

"Nabby Jonas, tall as a beanpole!" He laid the rest of his armload of handbills on the ground and weighted them down with a rock. "Move your thumb if you do not wish it nailed to the tree, too." Whack, whack, whack with the hammer. "Your mother is well?"

"My mother is dead," said Nabby, "and you never setting foot in our house for many a month after—"

After he had sworn eternal gratitude to Nabby's mother a few years ago for saving him, white-faced and terrified, from the Royal Navy's press gang. If she had not hidden him in the cubby under the stairs, he would have been bundled off to sea along with everybody else that moved along the waterfront that dark night. Will touched Nabby's shoulder.

"I am sorry, indeed," he said. "The printer to whom I have been apprenticed this six months gives me hardly a moment to myself. Run here, run there, work the press, nail up broadsides for the Sons of Liberty—" He snatched up his bundle. "Come along. You can help me."

"Can I indeed?" Nabby tossed her head. "I have business of my own."

She ran away before he could see the tears in her eyes. Hateful boy! Had he once asked how things fared for her? Did he care whether she was homeless and about to be apprenticed to a mantuamaker? He called after her, but she only ran faster. The wind was rising, and before long there would be rain, which, she hoped, would turn Will Truax's wretched broadsides into pulpy rags. She turned into Marlborough Street and slowed. Soon the rain would catch her, too, and, anyway, she must, willy-nilly, present herself to Master Pettigrew to learn her fate before nightfall.

There was no doubt how she would spend her last few hours of freedom. As she had done so often before, coming home a roundabout way from errands for her mother, she would walk past the pewterers' shops on Cornhill, Milk, and Back Streets. She would peer through cloudy, small-paned windows or, if she was lucky, through a half-open door, to watch the pewterer and his apprentices ladling hot metal into molds or smoothing a plate on the lathe.

Will Truax was lucky to be sent out around the town sometimes. The mantuamaker would doubtless keep Nabby always indoors with a needle in her hand, out of sight both of the pewterers' shops and Long Wharf with its continual bustle of ships and seamen and two-wheeled carts unloading cargoes for the merchants of Boston. Girls, it seemed, were destined only to sew and cook and care for small children and scrub and—her lips quivered—help their mothers tend shop.

"Unfair!" Nabby said angrily.

"That it is!" A tall man with one of Will Truax's broadsides in his hand looked briefly down at her and strode by to join a cluster of people in front of the Old South Meeting House. His next words, plainly not meant for Nabby, floated back to her. "The time has come, methinks, when men of courage must take matters into their own hands."

And girls of courage, too? Nabby stared after him. Did she dare? Did she *not* dare, considering the mantuamaker? Reaching into her pocket to touch the little porringer for luck, Nabby darted down Milk Street and rushed into the shop of Tobias Butler, Pewterer. An anxious-faced woman—Master Butler's wife?—looked at her from behind a counter sparsely laden with a few pewter plates, a handful of spoons, half a dozen porringers, and one glossy tankard so handsomely curved that Nabby stood gazing at it for a long delicious moment.

"Your mistress has sent you for the tankard?" the woman asked timidly. "My husband will wish you to take a message to her." She stepped to a narrow hallway leading to the workroom. Nabby stood on tiptoe, trying in vain to see over Mistress Butler's shoulder. "Tobias! The girl has come for the tulip tankard."

"The girl? What girl?" An angry voice rose above the whir of the lathe, which died into silence. "For a Butler tankard that took almost the last of my best metal, her ladyship sends a serving girl? Let her cool her heels then until I finish burnishing this plate."

Whir of lathe again, rattle of wheels as a carriage halted just outside, a bump and a wail from somewhere abovestairs—Mistress Butler looked desperately from street to stairs.

"My poor Emily! I must—"

"Shall I go, Mistress?" Nabby asked. "And soothe the child? Mayhap this is the lady for the tankard, for indeed I am not. Up yonder stairs?"

"I—" Mistress Butler was doubtful. "Tobias may be angry, but—"

"But you cannot be two places at once," Nabby

said briskly, "and milady, whoever she is, is alighting from her coach."

Mistress Butler fluttered to the door, curtsying. Nabby's lip curled. She would curtsy to no one, least of all to an idle lady in a carriage who was likely waited on hand and foot. Still, who but the gentry had money to buy so handsome a tankard?

Nabby pushed open the door at the head of the stairs. Sprawled on the pegged wooden floor, a girl, pale and tearful, looked up at her like an animal in a trap. Just out of reach, a pair of crutches had slid every which way across the floor. Poor Emily, indeed!

"I fell," she said in a muffled voice. "Who are you?"

"I am Nabby." She picked up the crutches. "Your mother is busy with a high-born lady."

"Yes." Emily was perhaps two years younger than Nabby, but her blue eyes had a hurt look that made her seem older than she was. "No, do not help me." She pulled herself up on the crutches and, with useless legs dangling, inched her way painfully to a chair. "They— my mother and father—are always busy." She sighed. "Where do you live?"

"On Long Wharf," said Nabby before she remembered that she lived nowhere now.

"Tell me what it is like there." Emily sank back against the cushions. "As you see, I do not fare abroad." Her voice turned bitter. "Chair and bed, bed and chair, God's will be done."

"How long?" Nabby asked pityingly.

"Five years." Emily's head drooped. "My only

brother died of it, a distemper for which even Dr. Joseph Warren, the physician, knew no cure, but I was left as you see me." She managed a watery smile. "Picture me Long Wharf, if you please."

Long Wharf—the peddlers awaiting the seamen with their bits of smuggled goods, a ship's cargo being unloaded and trundled off to nearby warehouses, bearded men telling tales of far places in the Widow Parsons' tobacco shop, the doors to the grog shops opening and closing to the sound of tumult within. It was all clear in Nabby's mind, but putting it into words was another matter.

"You have truly never seen the wharf?" she asked.

"Mayhap before the—the illness, but I do not remember."

"Very well, then," Nabby began hesitantly. "Long Wharf is part street and part wharf. On the street side my mother has—had—a little shop, with two small rooms abovestairs. Opposite our doorstep, the street becomes a wharf like any other." She paused. "One can lean out and look a ship in the face."

Emily's cheeks were flushed.

"Oh, I wish— But go on, please."

"This morning when I left, I saw a sailor with a parrot on his shoulder, and once a seaman came into the tobacco shop who had seen the king riding out in his coach in London. Another time—"

"You, girl!" Mistress Butler came clattering up the stairs. "All is well?"

"Thanks to Nabby," Emily said in a chilly voice. "She handed me my crutches, else I should have lain here helpless forever."

"But, child, the lady came for the tankard and—"

"And a tankard is more important than a daughter," Emily muttered.

Mistress Butler turned to Nabby. "I thank you for your help. Now, what brings you to our shop?"

"I wish to speak with Master Butler," Nabby said loftily, "on a matter of business."

"My husband is not to be troubled with trifles."

"This is not a trifle," said Nabby. It was, in fact, her whole future life.

"Come then," said Mistress Butler in a resigned voice.

"No!" Emily cried. "She was telling me about Long Wharf!"

Nabby touched her hand. "I will tell the rest of it later."

The blue eyes searched her face. "Promise?"

"Promise."

"Today?"

"I—I think so." Nabby turned her eyes resolutely away from Emily's pleading face. "But now I must speak with your father."

For whatever good it would do her. She feared that Tobias Butler would be no more agreeable to her becoming a pewterer's apprentice than Master Pettigrew was.

It was not, it seemed, an auspicious moment to inquire. Mistress Butler, with an air of throwing Nabby into a den of lions, pushed open the door to the workshop, muttered, "The girl would have a word with you," and scuttled back into the sales room.

Tobias Butler was a man to match his voice, large

and angry-looking. He was fuming at an inattentive boy who was languidly turning the big wheel that powered the lathe.

"Copper enough in Connecticut, to be sure, but lead far away in Virginia, and tin, which is the most important, hard to come by from Cornwall and high as a cat's back besides, with the British taxes laid on. I am aweary of trying to do a proper job with old melted-down pieces of pewterware and very few of those." He turned impatiently. "Well, girl?"

"Sir," said Nabby, "I wish to become an apprentice."

"And why not?" Nabby's heart leaped. "Boston is full of people who could accommodate an industrious girl, if so you are. A mantuamaker, mayhap." He looked critically at the plate. "Faster on the wheel, Lonzo. At this rate, we shall be at the burnishing all day long."

"Sir," said Nabby to his unresponsive back. "I wish to be a *pewterer's* apprentice."

He turned to stare, while the lathe whirred on.

"No, no! Already I am saddled with— A girl! Not to be thought of!"

"I am strong," said Nabby, "and I—I love pewter."

"You love pewter? And where did you learn to love pewter?"

Nabby forced herself to meet his sharp eyes.

"From looking into shops such as yours, sir. Also, I have a small porringer that my father, a seaman, brought me from England."

"What touch?" Master Butler demanded. Then,

at her blank look, "The mark on the back, girl. The touchmark."

"A rose and crown, sir."

He nodded. "And the handle? What design? Dolphin? Crown? Flowered? Ha, you do not know! And you say you love pewter!"

"It is because I do not know that I wish to become an apprentice and learn," Nabby said desperately.

He gave her a studying look. "Were you not a girl, I might— But no, you *are* a girl, and girls do not become pewterer's apprentices." He turned back to his work. "Be off with you, and"—his voice softened ever so little—"I wish you good fortune."

"Thank you, sir."

Nabby barely managed to keep her voice steady. All was lost here. She would try the Cornhill Street pewterer next, although she had had neither sup nor bite since her frugal breakfast of bread and cheese, and rain was rattling on the cobblestones. Besides, the time was slipping closer and closer to the hour when Master Pettigrew would expect her, to be viewed by the mantuamaker or the wigmaker or the flower woman.

There was a cry from abovestairs and then another —"She promised! She promised!"—and Mistress Butler burst into the workroom.

"Tobias, you have not sent that girl away? She has fair bewitched our Emily, who weeps for her—something about Long Wharf—and I fear she may do herself an injury." She caught sight of Nabby. "There you are, my girl! Pray hasten abovestairs and comfort the child."

Master Butler looked in bewilderment from his wife to Nabby and back again.

"I will go to her at once," said Nabby. "I did indeed promise to tell her tales of Long Wharf, although I must be away in a few moments lest Master Pettigrew—" She turned at the doorway. "Master Butler, pray consider that when the *Boston Traveller* makes port, which I think may be before nightfall, I might— if I wished—put you in the way of picking up some old pieces of pewter to be remelted as you said. Mayhap my friends would even be inclined to bring in a few ingots of tin at the end of the next voyage to England —if, that is, I spoke to them in your behalf."

"What's that?" Master Butler, openmouthed, stared after her. "What did you say?"

But Nabby was gone, up the steep stairs to the wailing Emily.

" 'Oh, Master Butler, I—I love pewter!' " Lonzo,
Tobias Butler's apprentice, let his voice rise to a mocking falsetto as Nabby ladled steaming codfish stew from
the black pot hanging on the kitchen crane. He yelped
as Nabby thumped the wooden trencher down in front
of him and splashed a gobbet of hot stew on his hand.
"Ow-w-w! You did that on purpose!"

"Did I?" Nabby turned an innocent face in his
direction. "Your lordship is accustomed to more skillful servants, mayhap?"

For all her pert answer, she was sick at heart. Were
it not for her, Master Butler would not now be melting
down the three battered pewter plates and eight bent
spoons that she had cajoled from her father's old shipmates under the peddlers' greedy eyes. Neither would
he have the promise of a few ingots of tin from Cornwall, if such could be had, which the bos'n, Silas
Bridges, would try to bring in on the next voyage of
the *Boston Traveller*—four weeks there and, with
luck, six weeks back. All of this—and for what?

With rising hope, Nabby had waited in a corner
of the Widow Parsons' tobacco shop while Master But-

ler and Silas Bridges had made their arrangements in a nearby grog shop. Around her the talk rose and fell as sailors fresh from the sea came to buy tobacco for their pipes.

"East India Company . . . four ships coming from England . . . tea to be taxed at threepence the pound . . . Sons of Liberty . . . a meeting at Faneuil Hall . . . the broadsides say . . . Sam Adams . . . taxation without representation . . ."

Obsessed with her own worries, Nabby had sat unheeding as the rain sluiced down the small-paned windows.

"All is arranged," said Master Butler when at last he returned to the tobacco shop, "and I thank you for your help."

"Then—"

"But I cannot take a girl as an apprentice, although methinks you have a true feel for pewter." His face darkened. "Unlike that numskull of a Lonzo."

"But—" Her head drooped. "Very well, sir. I must then betake myself at once to Master Pettigrew to be apprenticed elsewhere since I am an orphan with no roof over my head."

"An orphan? No roof?" Echoing her words, Master Butler sounded like the red-and-green parrot that a seaman had once brought into Nabby's mother's shop. "This I did not understand. Did we not leave Emily, amid tears, bidding you return to finish some story or other? Mayhap—" Again Nabby felt a great surge of hope. "Times are hard, but a man cannot do his best work with a weeping daughter and the household in an uproar. I will speak with Master Pettigrew at once."

Did this mean that he would take her as an apprentice after all? It did not. Instead, Nabby, exhausted and discouraged, had agreed to be bound out as a servant in the Butler household, dishing up stew and chowder and telling stories of Long Wharf to Emily, all for the sake of being close to where pewter was made. She sighed. Nearly two weeks gone, and she had yet to set foot in the workroom save to summon Tobias Butler and Lonzo to their meals. Each time when she had lingered, fascinated by brief glimpses of molds and metal, Mistress Butler or Emily had called her away.

Nabby frowned at thought of Emily. Every morning Master Butler alone or Nabby and Mistress Butler together, making a chair of their hands, carried her down the steep stairs to sit all day long in the kitchen back of the shop. Sometimes on bright days she hobbled painfully on her crutches to the outside door to peer out, but the curve of the street and looming Fort Hill cut off the view of the wharves along the waterfront.

To Nabby, accustomed to roaming the meandering streets of Boston, being caged inside was a sore trial. How much worse for poor Emily, who had no memories of Long Wharf's flurry and hustle to sustain her!

"Had we but a carriage," said Nabby, "or any other vehicle, we would be able to see the sights. Oh, such things as I would show you!"

Not only Long Wharf but Griffin's and Rowe's and a dozen others; Faneuil Hall topped by its great golden grasshopper; the Liberty Tree under whose spreading branches the Sons of Liberty held their noisy rallies; the scattering of tiny islands in the harbor; the

Common, where the cattle grazed and the militia drilled—Nabby ached to be out and away. Even life with the mantuamaker could hardly be more confining than this.

Nabby's only consolation was that here she could look at the pieces of pewter that Master Butler spread out for show on the counter—few enough but each perfect of its kind. The tulip tankard was gone, carried away by the lady in the carriage, but a tall coffeepot with rings of beading around lid, base, and body was left, besides a church chalice and a basin with a domed cover.

"The more fool, I!" Master Butler growled as he strode into the little sales room where Nabby was standing guard while Mistress Butler put Indian pudding to bake for long hours in the brick oven. "Plates, spoons, and mugs are the things that sell." He pointed a finger at Nabby. "Tell me then, girl, why I use my scarce metal on items that only the wealthy can buy."

"Mayhap," said Nabby, "because you cannot help yourself. My father could not but go to sea, although he could have bettered himself by working ashore."

Master Butler gave her a surprised look.

"An old head on young shoulders, methinks," he said. "A man must follow his bent, 'tis true, and do his best work come what may."

"Sir," said Nabby, greatly daring, "is it possible to find a way for your Emily to fare abroad? She does not thrive, shut up here like a—a chicken in its coop. Is she to live out her days with no more than a glimpse of the outside world?"

Startled, he glowered at her. "Are you not here to

tell her tales of the outside world, girl? Do you dream that I, a mere craftsman, can also afford a carriage in which my daughter can take the air?"

"Oh, no, sir! I only thought—"

But Master Butler was already stamping back to his workroom. Nabby frowned. If it had been his son who had lived, even as a cripple, Master Butler would have found a way fast enough to meet his needs. Nabby set her jaw. She would think of something for Emily sometime, somehow. A cart? Too heavy by far for Nabby to push, even if Master Butler had one and even if Emily could be made comfortable in it. A child's sled might be remodeled to do for a bit, but snow seldom lay long on the streets of Boston. Cold rain was the more common affliction. In any case, whatever Nabby thought of would cost money, and she had none. All she had of value in the world was her beautiful little porringer, which glowed on the table in the room that she shared with Emily. She jumped as the outside door banged open.

"You?" It was Will Truax again. "What do you here?"

Nabby hesitated. "I am indentured to Master Butler."

Will gaped at her. "As an apprentice? To a pewterer?"

"Nay. As a nursemaid and servant." Her look dared him to mock at her. "If I were a boy, Master Butler would have taken me at once. He says I have a—a feel for pewter."

"No doubt." He edged past her toward the workroom door. "I have a message for Master Butler."

"I can take it for him. He mislikes being disturbed when he is busy with the pewter."

"Mislike it or not—" Will shrugged. "Ah, well, I must still make my way to the cooper's and"—he shifted a sheaf of broadsides to consult a list in his hand—"the locksmith's and the hatter's and—" Did these people have no names? There were more than one of each occupation in Boston—a dozen, for all Nabby knew. Will's voice sank to a whisper. "Give Master Butler this message, for his ear alone: 'The Green Dragon, eight o'clock tonight.'" He whipped out a broadside. "And this as well."

"To be sure." Here was an excuse to go into the workroom and sniff the odor of molten metal and the forge fire that kept it that way. "Your master wants an answer?"

"No need. Master Butler will come or he will not, methinks."

Will was gone again, clattering down the street without another word. The Green Dragon—why the mystery about inviting Master Butler to a tavern that Nabby had passed many a time, with its rows of windows and its hammered copper dragon, turning greenish with time, suspended over the front door?

Nabby glanced down at the broadside in her hand —two broadsides, as it turned out, stuck together by the fresh ink. She folded the spare one to study at her leisure and thrust it into her pocket. Then she marched into the workroom. Master Butler, steady-handed, was ladling hot metal into a small opening in a two-piece brass mold hinged at one end and held tightly together with wooden handles at the other.

"Pay heed!" he was saying to Lonzo. "Not too hot, not too cold, either metal or mold. Never forget to coat the inside of the mold with egg white and red ocher first, lest we end up with metal and mold melted together into one." He glared at Lonzo. "No wool-gathering, boy! I doubt you have noted a word of this." He glanced up at Nabby, standing spellbound. "Well, girl, what now?"

"Is it to be a porringer, sir? And may I stay to see?"

"Only a plate this time, but watch a bit if you like. When the metal cools enough, I will take the plate from the mold—listen, Lonzo!—and melt off the tedge, which is the extra metal remaining around the edge, with a soldering iron. After that I will impress my mark on the bottom."

"The touchmark," Nabby said triumphantly.

"True for you. Lonzo, fetch the steel die for her to see. An anchor, with *T.B.* inscribed at the top and *Boston* at the bottom—not so fair as the rose and crown on your English porringer but more suited to my style."

Nabby clapped her hands to her mouth.

"Oh, sir, I forgot. I have a—a message." She glanced toward Lonzo. "For your ears alone."

"Lonzo, pray betake yourself to the shed and fetch more charcoal for the forge. Very well, girl."

"The printer's apprentice brought the message," Nabby muttered, scarlet with mortification. " 'The Green Dragon at eight o'clock tonight.' And I am to give you this."

She handed over the broadside. Master Butler looked at it, frowning.

"And so we must act, lest— Well, Nabby, why do you stand there? Are not my good wife and daughter in need of you?"

Nabby scuttled miserably back to the shop she was supposed to be tending. How could she have been so carried away by her interest in pewter as to forget her duty and anger Master Butler? She took the extra broadside out of her pocket, unfolded it on the counter next to a pair of pewter spoons, and pored over the words. When she was small, Nabby, like other little girls, had gone to the free school just long enough to learn reading and writing and simple sums. That was all the education most girls of Nabby's station in life ever got, but boys often went to school for years. Even apprentices were sent to evening schools for the learning required by their indentures—unfair again, Nabby thought angrily.

The broadside had a few long words, but, lips moving, Nabby was able to sound them out. They merely invited the freemen of Boston and other towns in the province to meet at the Liberty Tree on Wednesday at noon. At that hour the people to whom tea was being shipped from England were to appear and resign their offices "and swear that they will reship any tea by the first vessel sailing for London."

Mistress Butler emerged, breathless, from the kitchen.

"All goes well?" she asked, as though she feared the shop had been so crowded with customers demanding pewter that Nabby had had to turn some of them away.

"A message for Master Butler from the printer,"

said Nabby, "which I delivered to him. Also, one carriage, two carts, three small boys, and one dog passed on the street."

Mistress Butler gave her a hard look. "Too pert by far, my girl!"

"Indeed, such is not my intention," Nabby said meekly. "I deem it my duty to remember what I see so that I may tell Emily how the world wags outside."

She found Emily in her chair, staring gloomily at the fire. She brightened at the sight of Nabby.

"Here is a broadside that the printer's boy brought," said Nabby. "A meeting at the Liberty Tree, something about sending some tea back to England whenever it reaches port here."

Nabby suspected that Master Butler's meeting at the Green Dragon was about tea, too, but she uttered not a word about that. If she were to earn a reputation for reliability, she must leave Master Butler to do his own talking. Emily was not interested in meetings anyway. She merely glanced at the broadside and turned it over to the blank side.

"Paper!" she said in delight. "I have not had paper to draw on in many a day. Run, Nabby, and fetch me a bit of charcoal from the shed. The last piece rolled under the settle beyond my reach a month ago, and my mother swept it up when I was asleep. No matter, since I have had no paper since then anyway."

"You can draw?" asked Nabby in surprise.

"Yes. I can draw." Emily's voice, usually so soft, had a bite to it. "Not that anyone notes or cares."

"I do." Nabby hastened to fetch a piece of charcoal while Emily sat staring at the precious paper.

"I could draw a glimpse of the street from our doorway, but I have drawn that over and over for want of anything better."

"Your father's workroom?" asked Nabby, eager for any excuse to watch the pewtering herself.

" 'Tis so busy a place that I should only be in the way," Emily said uneasily. "Besides"—her face clouded—"my being there would only remind my father that he has no son to train in the skill."

"Tush!" said Nabby. "I have seen naught in that shop that a girl could not do, once she learned the tricks of the trade. 'Not too hot, not too cold,' and ladling the metal requires only a steady hand, as for chowder and stew."

Tears filled Emily's eyes. "Most girls could manage, but not I, tied to chair and bed as I am."

"I have it in mind to untie you one of these days." Nabby's voice was gentle. "For now, pray draw me the seaman with the parrot that I told you of."

The parrot, since Emily had never seen one, turned out to look rather like a goose, but the seaman was surprisingly like. Nabby immediately added paper as the second item on her mental list of needs for Emily. She doubted that Master Butler could supply it, for she had heard that it was expensive and not always easy to come by, anyway, but— Will Truax! Mayhap he could be persuaded to part with a few broadsides now and then. After all, the purpose of handbills was to inform the populace, and Nabby and Emily were as much part of the populace as anybody else.

As the days passed, broadsides flapped almost daily on the trunks of Boston trees, and Nabby looked hungrily out at them. Will Truax often brought messages, but now he insisted on speaking only to Master Butler. Once when Nabby was able to waylay him and ask for a few broadsides for Emily's drawings, he reluctantly passed over only a single sheet.

"Each one counts in times like these," he said. "It would be ill fortune were anyone to miss hearing of these urgent meetings."

"Surely you owe me a few of the scraps of paper that must be awasting in the print shop," said Nabby. "Pray remember that if it were not for my mother, you would not even be here tacking up broadsides but rocking on the sea in foreign parts."

In Nabby's opinion, there were worse things than that, but Will thought otherwise.

"Ships!" He shuddered. "I grow seasick even in a skiff on the harbor. Very well, then, I will try to find some odd bits of paper, though my master is a thrifty man who lets little go to waste. Also, he is as short-tempered as though he had pied a stick of type—especially now."

"I thank you," Nabby said airily, "and I beg you to think also of a means of transporting my master's Emily about Boston. She grows weary of being homebound and so, in truth, do I." She added a dab of honey to her request; after all this was for Emily, not for her. "A smart boy like you will know about such things."

"A smart boy, am I? Smart enough to know that a soft word from you may mean you are sickening with a fever." He grinned. "Mayhap I can think of something, once things are calm in Boston, which I fear will be on the far side of never."

It was true that Boston continued to seethe with

disquiet. The men to whom the expected tea was consigned flatly refused to resign. The militia was put on reluctant alert to deal with the riots and disturbances that had already resulted in property damage and danger to the tea interests. The selectmen called one town meeting after another and sent committees and individuals shuttling back and forth to the governor and the consignees in an effort to keep the tea from ever entering Boston. Master Butler was often from home, presumably attending meetings, while his own work was at a standstill. Mistress Butler watched the shop like a pale ghost, trading rumors and gossip with an occasional neighbor.

"Nabby, I have not enough meal for our supper mush," she said in a worried voice early on a Monday morning. "Tobias has been gone since barely dawn, and I dare not leave the shop. Pray go to the market in North Square and—"

"I have bought meal for my mother, many's the time." Nabby could hardly believe that she was actually to be sent out of the house on an errand. "Have no fear that I will not buy thriftily, Mistress."

If she ran all the way, she might have time to swing around by Long Wharf, either going or coming. She might even get up her courage to ask for paper at the print shop where Will Truax worked and where the *Boston Gazette,* urging the colonies to resist British taxation, was published every Monday.

"I will note everything I see," Nabby whispered to Emily, "and mayhap I can bring back a surprise for you as well."

She was tempted by a crisp broadside fluttering

on a tree not far from Long Wharf. "Friends! Brethren! Countrymen!"—plainly it was another of the deluge of handbills with which the Committee of Corresponddence,the Loyal Nine, or the Sons of Liberty were deluging Boston. Surely one would never be missed. She was about to pull it off the tree when she noted a drawing of a hand pointing to the words: "Show me the man who dares take this down." She drew back as though she had been burned, but a hand reached over her shoulder, yanked down the broadside, crumpled it into a ball, and sent it flying to the gutter. Nabby turned to look into the red face of a portly man who was gobbling with anger like a turkey.

"These rascally colonials! The governor should ship them all in chains to England to be dealt with as they deserve!"

"And what a fleet of ships it would take to transport all those who protest England's unjust dealings!" Nabby sputtered.

The man lifted a threatening hand, but Nabby ducked away and ran down the street, scooping up the broadside as she went. It might yet be smoothed out enough for Emily's use.

Nabby fled up Milk Street to Marlborough, where more people than she had ever seen in one place before were pushing their way into the Old South Meeting House. She veered around them and hurried to the market. Stowing the corn meal for Mistress Butler in her basket, she headed for the print shop. She stole a sideways look at the Green Dragon, but it appeared as silent and empty as though it were Sunday morning.

Through the dusty window of the printer's she

saw Will Truax, with his red hair hidden under a round knitted cap, pulling with all his might on the long wooden handle of the press. A man with a cocked hat set on the back of his head, a clay pipe in his mouth, and a worried expression was inspecting some recently printed sheets. This, Nabby decided, was no time to ask for paper, although she could see a few sheets lying on the floor.

Instead, she rushed to Long Wharf, where it seemed that all the people of Boston who had not been able to crowd into the Old South Meeting House were milling about like a herd of bewildered cattle. Carts and drays unloading cargo from a newly arrived ship must push their way through with shouts and warnings. Even the entrance to the Widow Parsons' tobacco shop, where Nabby had planned to stop, was blocked. Everyone was looking toward Castle William, two miles down the harbor. Nabby pushed her way to the end of the wharf.

"What betides?" she demanded of anyone who would listen.

"You have not heard?" A grizzled seaman handed her a spyglass. "Stale news, maid, for she was sighted yesterday."

Squinting through the glass, Nabby could make out a three-master anchored astern of the Admiral's flagship under the eyes of the British soldiery stationed at Castle William.

"What ship is that, then?" she asked.

"The *Dartmouth*, my girl," the sailor growled, "with an unwelcome cargo of tea for Boston. Now, methinks, the fat is in the fire."

"*Put my touchmark on that botched-up piece of* work? Never!" Master Butler's voice roared out from the workroom. "With a dozen small holes to fill by dripping pewter into them, 'twould be a patchwork job at best and a disaster at worst!"

Emily and Nabby, knitting stockings by the kitchen fire, could hear a murmur of complaint from Lonzo.

"Nay, boy! 'Good enough' does not merit Tobias Butler's touchmark. That is my signature, a pledge of my skill and my honor. Never must it go on shoddy work." Silence for a moment. "A scowl mends nothing. It was an error on my part to deem you more advanced in the craft than you are. We must melt this piece down and start again from the beginning, and this time hold the mold together with all your strength."

Nabby and Emily exchanged glances. Of late, Master Butler had the disposition of a bear with a thorn in his paw. He had been attending meetings almost daily and also taking his turn standing guard over the two tea ships, the *Dartmouth* and the lately arrived *Eleanor*, now anchored at Griffin's Wharf, a little south of Fort Hill.

The governor had flatly refused to allow the tea to be sent back to England. The selectmen, equally determined, had thereupon ordered a volunteer guard of citizens to prevent the tea, with its hated tax, from being taken ashore, although the captains were permitted to unload other cargo that the merchants of Boston would need to carry them through the long winter.

"And what did I get from their holds myself?" Master Butler had complained as he sat with the family and Nabby in the kitchen one evening after Lonzo had eaten and disappeared. "None of the tin I asked for and lead priced almost beyond my reach." A glance at Nabby. "If your man Silas Bridges and his shipmates are indeed able to bring me even a few ingots of tin, I will judge it a godsend, though it be smuggled goods. But how could Boston have survived these many years under Britain's repressive laws without some tax-free items now and then?"

Nabby, like most of Boston and many of the British customs officers, took smuggling quite for granted. Besides the ships from foreign ports, she had often watched the wood boats bringing in fuel for Boston from the countryside, sometimes with only a thin layer of kindling laid over something quite different.

"I have lost a stitch at the turn of the heel." Nabby, ever an inattentive knitter, dragged her thoughts reluctantly back from smuggling and tea and tin and Master Butler's reproaches still sounding thunderously from the workroom.

"Give me the stocking," said Emily, "and I will pick up the stitch for you." She handed her own knitting to Nabby. "Straight ahead for a bit."

"I thank you. What would I do without you to make right my mistakes? Lucky the mantuamaker who did not get me for an apprentice!" The needles clicked as Nabby frowned over her work. "Were I a pewterer, what touch should I choose, Emily?"

"Not the rose and crown of your porringer?"

"Nay. Roses and crowns are not for me. I think mayhap a ship—an honest trading ship like the *Boston Traveller,* riding the waves with all sails set. And on the prow *A.J.* for Abigail Jonas, for who would pay heed to a pewterer called Nabby?"

"I would," said Emily. "I would drive up in my carriage, walk into the shop with my silk skirts swishing, and order all kinds of things—a teapot and a coffeepot and a pair of candlesticks and an inkstand and a sugar bowl, three ladles and a dozen plates."

"I thank you for your patronage," said Nabby. "I will be rich indeed."

She would neither be rich nor mayhap even a pewterer, she sometimes feared, and poor Emily would never walk, but a dream now and then was a comfort if it did not take her mind away from more important matters. Helping her mother scramble for a meager living, she had always had to keep her thoughts mostly on hard facts and hard work.

"Some paper for you." Will Truax, with a cloth-wrapped bundle under his arm, stepped inside to hand a few rather worn handbills to Emily. "And some business to transact with Master Butler."

Nabby nodded. "Go then and transact it, and our thanks for the paper."

Mistress Butler came hurrying in from the shop. "Pray, what's the news, boy? Tobias is so much from home and so hurried when he *is* here that we hear almost nothing. Besides, like all men, he keeps his own counsel."

"The brig *Beaver,* third of the tea ships, has arrived," said Will, "but with smallpox aboard, so she is moored at Rainsford Island until the contagion has passed. The selectmen have instructed the captain to bring the tea from between decks and let it air all day when the weather is fair but on no account to permit one leaf of it to be landed."

"I would not buy such tea and risk catching the disease," said Mistress Butler.

"Nor any other tea"—Master Butler, appearing from the workroom, spoke sternly over her shoulder—"since all has taken on the flavor of tyranny. You have a message for me, boy?"

Will thrust the bundle at him. "My master begs you to repair this teapot. One of the legs has broken off and must be soldered on again. You will find it, he says, tucked away inside the pot. And can it be returned ere nightfall, for he will then have need of it?"

"Who comes to sup at your master's?" asked Nabby. "No less a one than the governor, methinks."

"Small chance of that." Master Butler gave her a severe look. "And pray hold your tongue. This is no affair of yours."

Nabby reddened. "I ask your pardon, sir. 'Tis said

that curiosity killed the cat, and I should not wish it to do the same for me."

Master Butler almost smiled. "You are too quick with an answer by far, though the answer be an apt one."

He began to unwrap the bundle, but Will Truax held up a warning hand.

"Best unwrap it on your worktable, sir. There may also be repairs to be made to the lid, which could —uh—roll off and be dented."

Master Butler nodded. "Forewarned is forearmed, they say."

He headed back to his workroom, where he could be heard shouting for Lonzo to deliver a pewter nursing bottle and a candlestick at once to Mistress Nicely at her house on School Street. Will Truax left, and Mistress Butler betook herself next door to pass her bits of news on to her neighbor.

"Now what was that nonsense with the teapot?" Nabby asked, but Emily, already sketching with her stub of charcoal on the back of one of Will's handbills, paid her no heed. "I do not believe that Will Truax's master would serve tea, of all things, in times like these, so why the haste for the return of the teapot?"

She was still puzzling over that an hour later, with three more stitches dropped, when Master Butler came out of his workroom with what Nabby supposed was the teapot, wrapped in the same piece of cloth as before.

"That rascally Lonzo has not yet returned," he grumbled, "which may be just as well, for he cannot be relied on to do anything right. Nabby, pray return

this to the printing office as fast as may be—you know the place?—and with care, mind you. Give it to Master Edes and to no one else, not even his apprentice, likely boy though he is. I would go myself, save that I have promised a porringer for tomorrow and have not had a moment even to choose the design."

"Yes, sir." Nabby ran to take her cloak and hood from their peg on the wall. "You will tell Mistress Butler that I am from home at your orders?"

"She is still from home, too, I fear, nattering with the neighbors."

"Then you will take heed for Emily, sir?"

He threw up his hands. "You will make a nagging wife for some luckless youth, young Nabby. Have no fear. I will even carry Emily into my workroom and set her in a corner out of harm's way."

Emily looked up, face glowing. "Will you, truly? I shall take my bits of paper and sit as still as a mouse, making sketches."

"Sketches? Sketches of what?"

"Of you, Father, and of the workroom, for I misremember your tools after—after this long while."

Nabby looked at her pityingly. Nabby's father, even away as much as he had always been, had noted her doings when he was between voyages, but Master Butler seemed not even to know of Emily's sketches.

"She has a gift, sir," said Nabby, "of which you can well be proud."

Master Butler gave his daughter a troubled look. "Away then, Nabby, with an easy mind. Indeed, a household of women brings naught but care to a busy man."

It was on the tip of Nabby's tongue to point out that a household of women also kept him fed and clothed and free to work uninterrupted at his craft, but she feared pushing his temper too far. She fairly flew out the door with the bundle under her arm, determined to do the task Master Butler had set her without the least error. She was doing what by rights an apprentice should be doing, was she not? If this, why not something else sometime until she might even learn some of the craft that Master Butler was trying to teach Lonzo?

As usual these days, there was much coming and going near the Old South Meeting House just across the way from Province House, where the governor, now at his country home in Milton, away from the uproar, had been accustomed to wrangle with his balky council. Nabby, bent on being trustworthy, did not pause an instant to listen, but she could not help catching a sentence here and there from men gathered in little groups to exchange rumors and gossip.

"Not a pair of pistols to be had in the whole town, and my wife shudders at every sound she hears."

"If the duty be not paid by midnight Thursday, the customs officers will confiscate the tea and unload it in spite of all."

"What a coil, with the governor, the customs men, the consignees, and the townspeople all at loggerheads!"

Nabby hurried on, shifting the awkward bundle from one arm to the other, so that the cloth in which the teapot was wrapped slipped a little. She set it down beside a high hedge to rewrap it and could not resist a look at the shining pewter. It was a fair piece of work indeed, with fat, comfortable curves and three hoof-type feet, all now in good repair.

Holding the lid carefully in place, Nabby turned the pot over to see if it bore Master Butler's touch-mark. It did not; instead, there was a rose and crown rather like the mark on Nabby's porringer. An English import, then? Turning the pot upright again, Nabby heard a rustle inside. She lifted the lid and peered in— a slip of paper with a column of writing, mayhap the bill for Master Butler's services.

"How now, maid? What are you doing beside a hedge with teapot in hand?"

Nabby jumped as a pair of women with market baskets on their arms paused to stare at her. She hastily bundled the teapot into its wrappings.

"I am delivering it f-for my master, the p-pew-terer," she stammered, "and the wrapping slipped." She ducked her head. "I bid you good day."

She ran, cloak flying, as though the town watch were after her. Resolving to glance neither to left nor to right, even if a fire-breathing dragon flew past her nose, Nabby reproached herself all the way to the printing office. If Master Butler should find out—but he would not find out. With downcast eyes, she delivered the teapot to Master Edes, who unwrapped it and set it on the press.

"There is a—" Nabby was about to mention the slip of paper inside but caught herself just in time. "I will tell my master that I gave it into your own hand."

"Do," Master Edes said absently, "and give him my thanks for his speedy response."

Nabby cast a yearning glance in the direction of

Long Wharf as she walked soberly home. The Widow Parsons would be full of gossip garnered from the seamen—gossip that Mistress Butler would no doubt receive with joy. At Griffin's Wharf, just as close to home, Nabby would be able to take a close look at the tea ships. Still, she had best not loiter anywhere lest Master Butler think her as feckless as Lonzo. It had been great good luck that the two women had not called out the watch to make sure Nabby had not stolen the teapot, but bad luck that they had put her to flight before she had had time to read the slip of paper inside.

Passing the cooper's, Nabby paused a moment to sniff the fresh scent of wood and to look at an assortment of barrels, kegs, and piggins. When she was small, her father, ever ingenious, had contrived a chair for her out of an old barrel that he had found cast away on the wharf with part of the side stove in. By cutting away some of the staves midway and attaching a barrelhead halfway down for a seat, he produced a cozy refuge for a little maid. The sides had curved around to keep the cold drafts from her, and the back had made a place to lean her head. She blinked. Enough of that. Memories of a chair made out of a barrel would help her not at all in becoming a pewterer.

A carelessly dressed man with a seamed face and an air of determination was going into the Old South Meeting House with a train of followers as Nabby passed.

"Sam Adams," a man said behind her, "with new schemes to best the governor and rid us of this plaguey tea, methinks."

Will Truax was loitering at the edge of the crowd.

"The teapot has been returned to your master," Nabby murmured. A sudden notion struck her. "Did you also take a piggin to the cooper to be repaired? And a hat to the hatter? And a clock to the clockmaker?"

Will gaped at her, but she swished past him without another word. She had found out nothing, but she could not help suspecting that a message had been sent and another returned in the teapot. Mayhap it was only the roster for the guard on the tea ships, but there was no need for secrecy about that. Everybody in Boston, the British no doubt included, knew of the guard and what men were in it.

At home, Nabby found Mistress Butler minding the shop again and Emily happily sketching in the kitchen. This time, though, she was drawing the workroom—the lathe with its great driving wheel, the molds and burnishing tools, and the forge with its hood to guide the smoke upward.

"I watched while my father poured the metal for a porringer," she said proudly, as though Master Butler had conferred a great favor. Nabby sniffed. He could hardly have prevented Emily from seeing, since she was there in the room the whole time.

"And the handle too?"

Nabby wanted very much to learn the different kinds of handles for porringers, but mayhap her chance would come.

" 'Twas not like yours." Emily sketched busily and handed over a scrap of paper. "Dolphin, he called it."

Indeed, two dolphins were entwined on the handle with a plain shield between. Emily put aside her drawings with a sigh.

"And so I am without paper again," she said ruefully, "but it was one of the best afternoons of my life."

Not for paper alone, Nabby was sure, but for being allowed in the workroom with her father for the first time since who knew when. Nabby blessed Lonzo for not returning on time and Mistress Butler for going to gossip with the neighbors. Otherwise, this would have been a humdrum day for Emily, as well as for Nabby, who had been set free to scamper through the town.

Master Butler was from home that evening, attending what Will Truax, buttonholed by Mistress Butler the next day as he passed on one of his endless errands, described as an overflow mass meeting with delegates from five surrounding towns.

"And all determined not to allow a single leaf of tea to be unloaded," he said. "If the British continue to be as stubborn as we, anything can happen."

Master Butler was bent on errands most of the following day, too, although he did bide in his workroom long enough to finish the porringer, which he sent Lonzo to deliver. Nabby wished he had sent her, for just from watching the street outside, she could sense the excitement in the town.

On the Thursday, with a chilly rain falling, all manner of men—merchants, seamen, artisans, craftsmen—hurried up Milk Street to the meeting house. The gathering appeared to last all day, for Nabby, sent by Mistress Butler to buy a bit of sugar—"and pray try to bring us some news, even though it delay your return"—saw only a few people leaving the meeting, where, a passerby told Nabby, Sam Adams and Dr. Warren had been speaking at length. One messenger, doubtless carrying another demand from the meeting to the governor in Milton, galloped away on horseback toward Boston Neck, the narrow strip of land that kept Boston from being entirely surrounded by water—and then only at low tide. Wet and cold, Nabby came home soon after four when the sky was clearing a little and the sun already setting. She hurried into the warm kitchen to relay her news, what little there was of it.

"A northwest wind," she said, shivering, "and colder than ever."

"Fetch yourself a bowl of mush from the hearth," Mistress Butler said. "Tobias has already supped, as though he knew not whether he ate fish or corn husks. He is now in his workroom with the door barred, but methought a moment ago that I heard muffled voices as though others had entered through the outside door beside the shed."

Nabby looked at her with astonishment. She could not remember Master Butler's ever allowing outside visitors in his workroom. He could barely endure even Lonzo's presence for all his need of help.

"Not only that," Mistress Butler continued in an aggrieved voice, "but I am to remain abovestairs as soon as I make sure that you and Emily are abed, as early as may be. No foot, he said, is to cross our threshold before daybreak."

"Where is Lonzo?" Nabby wondered idly.

"I heard Tobias tell him to take his candle and

keep to his room, for he would have no need of him tonight."

Lonzo, whose evenings were supposed to be his own, would not like being cooped up in his cubbyhole of a room, walled off from the shed where metal, charcoal, and wood for the kitchen fireplace were stored. Nabby, ever curious about people, had found out nothing about Lonzo except that he was the son of a carpenter from the North End, dead some years ago.

Nabby and Mistress Butler carried Emily upstairs, with her drawings clutched in her hand. Then Nabby ran back down to fetch the warming pan, with its coals from the hearth.

"I bid you good night," said Mistress Butler. "Pray do not burn the candles needlessly. The night is for sleeping."

With that last admonition, she retired to her own chamber, obviously irked at being sent off to bed like a child. Nabby settled Emily in bed with her crutches on the floor beside her and looked out through the branches of the tree that framed the diamond-paned window. A young moon did little to dispel the outside darkness, and a cold wind crept in around the window frame. Still, Nabby did not change into her night rail and seek the comfort of her bed. Instead, she sat staring at her precious porringer, agleam in the candlelight.

"Strange things are afoot tonight, methinks," she said.

"I feel it, too," Emily quavered. "Those broadsides on which I sketch threaten fearsome things."

"But naught can touch us here, safe in this sturdy

house." Nabby tucked the porringer under her pillow, a talisman for happy dreams. "Count over the good things of this day, and sleep well."

"I will, but—oh!"

Feet thudded down the street, and a tumult of shouts and whooping as of a whole tribe of angry Indians echoed through the darkness.

Nabby threw open the casement window, heed-
less of the blast of cold air that swept through the room.
By leaning out perilously far and craning her neck almost out of joint, she could see dark figures rushing
down Milk Street from the direction of the Old South
Meeting House, whooping as they went.

"Whoever they are, they are bound for the harbor," she said, "mayhap down Hutchinson Street to
Griffin's Wharf." She snatched up her hooded cloak.
"Pretend to be sleeping, Emily, in case your mother
comes to inquire." She hastily stuffed two of the cushions from Emily's chair under her own bedcover.
"There, is it not a fair likeness of me asleep?" She blew
out the candle and tiptoed to the door. "Why, 'tis
locked!"

"Then you must stay here," Emily said in a re-
lieved voice.

"So it seems, unless—" Nabby looked specula-
tively at the tree just outside the window. "Emily, if
you can close the window behind me to keep out the
cold and open it again when I return, I can easily climb
down the tree and see what betides."

49

"Pray, Nabby, do not go." Emily's voice was pleading. "My father—"

"Your father will know naught of it, I promise you, unless you tell."

"I would never tell, but you might fall, and then no one would need to tell."

"I will not fall. I have balanced myself many a time on the deck of the *Boston Traveller* tossing at anchor just opposite our door. Besides, think of what I will be able to tell you—exciting things for your sketches."

"Y-yes." Emily struggled out of bed and reached for her crutches. "You will take care, lest—"

"Lest a wandering bear devour me. Indeed, Emily, I shall skulk from shadow to shadow in my dark cloak, and no one will know I am there."

Through the window and down the tree—it was only a few moments until she was standing on the ground looking up at the white blur of Emily's face. The window closed with the faintest click of the latch. Nabby crept toward the street, keeping close to the wall of the house. No light shone from Master Butler's workroom now. He and his mysterious visitors must have fared forth to see what befell in the street, still noisy with whoops, yells, and whistles.

"Let me out! Let me out!"

Nabby shrank against the wall as Lonzo's muffled voice came to her from the shed room. So he, too, was locked in, but if he had not wit enough to climb out of his own window, he deserved to stay there. She hoped that he, of all people, had not seen her but was only calling out to anybody who might hear. She shivered from cold and excitement but not at all from fear. She was tall and strong and fleet of foot, and she knew every turn of the streets hereabouts.

She peered cautiously around the corner of the house. She was just in time to see, by the pale light of the waning moon, an apprentice climbing down from a nearby roof, apparently smearing soot from the chimney on his face as he went—a strange thing to do, but there had been many strange happenings in Boston of late.

Trying to be invisible, Nabby dodged along the darkest part of the street toward Fort Hill, where the shouts seemed loudest. There a squad of men, ghostly in the shadows, marched smartly past, to be joined by clumps of hurrying stragglers from the lanes and byways. Nabby followed to Griffin's Wharf, aswarm with indistinct figures milling around the tea ships—three of them, now that *Beaver* had been moved out of quarantine to join *Dartmouth* and *Eleanor*. Nabby melted into the shadow of a warehouse to watch in silence with a gathering crowd of men, women, and a few children.

By the flare of scattered torches, whose flames flickered in the wind, Nabby could see that men in outlandish attire were clambering aboard the tea ships. Bandannas, hoods, mufflers, and knit caps were pulled well down to disguise grim faces striped and smeared in black, red, and various shades between. Master Butler would have used charcoal from the forge or the red ocher with which he prepared his molds, if indeed he were here at all. Somehow Nabby could not imagine him whooping like an Indian, with his face streaked with war paint. The light caught the shine of hatchets, and an occasional pistol was stuck pirate-style in a sash or belt. Nabby edged to leeward of a large woman whose bulk would shelter her from a freshening breeze with a feel of icicles in it.

"Hast heard, maid, that the fourth tea ship, the brig *William,* is aground on Cape Cod in a gale?" an old man leaning on a blackthorn stick muttered in Nabby's ear. "One less batch of tea for our stalwart lads to deal with!"

Nabby had not long to wait to see how the stalwart lads were planning to deal with the tea. Clearly in undisputed possession of the ships, men were hauling the tea chests up from the holds by slings and cranes. Hatchets flashed as the chests with their burlap coverings were ripped open and the tea flung overboard.

"At 'em, boys! Leave never a leaf!" the old man cackled gleefully. "Tea and sea water will make a brew fit for a king—King George himself!"

The whole operation, guided by quiet orders from the men on shipboard, was as precise as though each man had been drilled in what he was expected to do. Plainly, this was no sudden outburst of anger like some of the riots of recent weeks.

On the deck of the *Dartmouth,* Nabby caught a flash of red hair straying from under a bandanna with a turkey feather stuck jauntily through the knot. Will Truax, neatly striped with printer's ink, was busily flinging the shattered chests into the sea, where they bobbed on the water like wrecks of children's play-boats. Nabby's father had once told her that, while Long Wharf could handle the largest seagoing vessels, the harbor at Griffin's Wharf was never more than a

few feet deep. Now, with the tide near its lowest ebb, the three ships looked to be almost aground. As the tea was tossed over the side, it began to build up like beehives in the shallow water.

"You, there, boy! Find some of your fellows and make sure the tea is well awash."

Nabby stared, wide-eyed. It was the unmistakable voice of Master Butler, whose face was decorated with slashes of red ocher under a sloppy turban remarkably like the patched old apron that Mistress Butler wore when she scrubbed the wide boards of the kitchen floor. He and his mysterious visitors must have been busy in the workroom the whole time disguising themselves for this foray.

" 'Tis ill that it must be done at low tide," the gaffer with the blackthorn stick gabbled on, "but all must be finished by midnight, they say, else the customs men will take possession."

Nabby nodded impatiently at news she already knew. She edged closer to the plump woman, pleasantly scented with cinnamon, while the old man smelled only of tobacco and stale beer. The dim little moon had set by now, and some of the flares were burning out. Still, Nabby could see a group of boys jumping with joyous whoops onto the piled-up tea in the water and tossing it to the wind. There would be many a case of chills and fever tomorrow, but who paid heed to that on such a night?

In the confusing swirl of motion ashore, on deck, and asea, Nabby lost track of Master Butler and Will Truax. A few men swept the decks, and others saw that the last broken tea chests were pushed well away from the shallows. A brief uproar arose on the wharf as three men wrestled another to the ground, removed his coat, and emptied something out of his pockets into the water.

"Be off with you!" one of them shouted. "And think yourself lucky that we do not replace your coat with one of tar and feathers!"

"A fair return for filling his pockets with tea!" the old man murmured.

Someone called the apprentices in from their chore of drowning the tea in sea water. The "Indians" began to leave, some forming into groups and others slipping away by twos and threes into the darkness.

"A good night's work! December 16, 1773, will be long remembered." The cinnamon-scented woman spoke her first words of the evening and turned to lumber away, leaving Nabby exposed to a wind that was colder than ever. "No doubt we will pay dearly for it, too, but methinks it will be worth the price."

To Nabby's experienced eye, the tide was on the turn now, washing the tea closer to shore—no matter now, though, since it was well soaked with salt water. Enthralled with the scene, Nabby had quite forgotten that time was passing and that Master Butler might already have left for home. Whether or no, she must rush away at once. If she hurried, she would have time to climb safely into bed before he could remove his war paint and come abovestairs to check on his presumably sleeping household.

She ran at top speed through the lanes to Milk Street, hiding in the shadows from any other night travelers, although all seemed as anxious as she not to be seen. She clambered up the tree like a cat, tapped ever so softly on the window, and tumbled breathlessly into the room the moment the waiting Emily flung open the casement window.

"Safe," Nabby whispered, "thanks to you!" She rubbed Emily's cold hands with her own icy ones. "You have not caught a chill waiting for me? I will tuck you warm in your bed again and perch alongside wrapped in my quilt, for what a tale I have to tell!"

She would almost have thought her tale was merely a dream that had vanished with the day except that Master Butler, eating his mush and milk in gloomy silence the next morning, had a small smear of red at the edge of his hair and a pair of damp boots drying by the fire. Lonzo, sullen-faced, sat picking at a torn pocket of his coat, a much-darned castoff.

"Off with your coat," Mistress Butler said in a resigned voice, "and Nabby will mend the pocket for you."

Lonzo muttered something about having a candlestick to deliver.

"You took that yesterday." Master Butler roused himself from a brown study.

Lonzo angrily passed the coat to Nabby.

"I will wait, then, while you stitch it up."

"You will not wait," said Master Butler. "You will go at once and make up the fire in the forge. You will not need a coat for that or for aught else today. We have the final buffing to do on a pair of mugs, after which I will go to the brass founders to inspect some new molds."

"Molds for what, sir?" Nabby could not resist asking.

"A dram bottle for use," Master Butler said with a wry face, "and a pear-shaped teapot for beauty."

"More teapot molds?" Mistress Butler ventured. "With not a leaf of honest tea to be had in all of Boston?"

"And a pot-bellied creamer," he went on.

So it was going to be business as usual, as though last night had never been.

"Do not fear," Master Butler told his wife. "If I cannot come by some tin soon, I will be making nothing either for use or beauty." He halted Nabby as, with Lonzo's coat tucked under her arm, she prepared to go abovestairs for needle and thread. "How long before we may expect the *Boston Traveller* to return to port?"

Nabby shrugged. "Wind and weather play a part, sir." This was a fact of which Master Butler and everybody else in Boston were well aware. "The ship is not a fast one, she must often wait long in port for a return cargo, and the winter storms are to be feared." She counted on her fingers. "She left Long Wharf the second week in November, and 'tis now December 17. Oh, sir, she can hardly return before the last of January."

He nodded gloomily. "So I feared. Well, we must still make do with pewter melted down from old pieces and hope to improve the alloy by adding small bits of this and that. The Worshipful Company of Pewterers in London is happy to ship chests of completed pewter pieces to the colonies to be sold, but they make sure that local craftsmen do not have the raw materials needed to make our own—another grievance to add to the ones we already have."

"Pray, sir," Nabby said demurely, "have you news of what befell last night? There was a great whooping and shouting in the street."

Master Butler gave her a sharp look. "The talk is that a tribe of Indians boarded the tea ships and threw all the tea into Boston Harbor."

Mistress Butler gave a little shriek. "Indians? Oh, Tobias, 'tis well that you forbade us to stir across the threshold."

And locked them in, to make doubly sure. Nabby let her glance stray thoughtfully to Master Butler's face.

"Sir, I fear you have hurt yourself. There is a red streak just—"

Mistress Butler fluttered to him. "Oh, Tobias, shall I fetch a cobweb to draw out the soreness?"

"No, woman, no!" Master Butler roared his way to the door. "I mislike this fretting and fussing over nothing—a brier scratch, at worst."

Nabby slid behind his back and abovestairs. What ever had possessed her to bait him in that fashion? Curiosity as to what he might reply was part of it, but also a wish to hear his version of last night's adventures. The only thing she had found out was that he did not intend to reveal his presence at the Boston Tea Party.

She sat down on the bed and sewed up Lonzo's pocket, taking care to reinforce the cloth underneath, which had been torn, too, as though caught on a splinter. She also checked the condition of the other pocket, not because she wished to oblige Lonzo but because care on this chore might convince Master Butler that she was a girl who could do painstaking work of other kinds as well.

As she turned the coat about, a sprinkling of something fell to the floor—a few leaves of tea, as she lived and breathed! So Lonzo had attended the tea party last night, too, ripping his coat as he broke out of his room. Nabby frowned. The tea leaves could mean that he had tried to make off with a whole pocketful of the stuff but had hastily disposed of it when he saw what befell the man who had been threatened with a coat of tar and feathers. Why, then, his reluctance to hand over the coat to be mended?

Nabby laid it out flat on the floor and felt over every inch of it. Not much to her surprise, a flat cloth-wrapped packet tied with twine was thrust deep into the ripped lining of the sleeve. She turned the package over and over in her hand, but curiosity was too much for her. She hurriedly undid the packet, which contained more tea, enough for many a cheering cup for those who could stomach the brew these days, mayhap the wives of British officials in town or of officers stationed at Castle William. Nabby stirred the leaves with her finger—bohea, the black tea much favored in Boston before true patriots gave up drinking it entirely.

So now what? In her hand Nabby held the means of ridding the household of Lonzo. Master Butler might overlook his sneaking out to attend the tea party, but he would never forgive his scooping up some of the hated tea and, Nabby felt sure, selling it wherever he might. With Lonzo gone, Nabby might have a chance to take his place, except— Except that she was a girl, and Master Butler was not yet ready to accept a girl as an apprentice, if indeed he ever would be.

Nabby picked up her little porringer, shimmering in the sun, and turned it over to admire the touchmark. Unwillingly she remembered Master Butler's words: "The touchmark is a pledge of my skill and my honor." Of skill Nabby had none, but honor— Her face clouded. Eager as she was to become a pewterer some day, she would never be able to look with pride at the touchmark she had chosen for herself, the sturdy sailing ship, if she got her start by bearing tales against even the shiftless Lonzo.

All the same, she would make sure that he did not profit from his pilfering. She opened the window and tossed the tea into a brisk breeze that scattered it over three rooftops. Then she tiptoed down the stairs, making sure to skip the step that creaked, and peered into the kitchen, where Emily sat alone. With a finger at her lips, Nabby climbed onto a settle and took down one of the bunches of parsley that Mistress Butler had hung from the rafters to dry, along with various other herbs for medicinal tea and flavoring. Nabby darted back upstairs, rubbed the dark dried parsley between her hands to the consistency of tea leaves, and tied it up in the packet, which she put back into Lonzo's sleeve lining.

"Here is your coat, as good as new!" she announced cheerily at the doorway to the workroom. "You will hardly know it was torn."

Lonzo, turning the wheel for Master Butler, gave her a suspicious look and no thanks.

"Lay it on the bench there," he said.

"Mind your manners!" Master Butler was stern. "A word of thanks ne'er comes amiss."

Nabby did not wait to hear it but went back to whisper the whole story to Emily in the chimney corner, while Mistress Butler, back from a gossip with the neighbors, tended the shop, now more scantily stocked than ever. Master Butler had paid dearly for the hours he had spent at meetings, where Nabby was sure that every detail of the tea party had been readied for use in case the negotiations among the governor, the tea consignees, and the town meeting came to naught. Now he must devote himself to pewtering again to make up for lost time.

Will Truax came with spare broadsides for Emily's drawings and paused to warm himself by the kitchen fire and relay the latest news.

"Master Butler has told you what befell the tea? This morning 'tis a strange sight indeed, for the high tide has washed it down the shore like drifts of seaweed."

Emily smiled. "I shall draw it so, then, as well as making a sketch of you, Will Truax, standing on the deck of the *Dartmouth* tossing the tea chests over the side." She clapped her hands over her mouth and gave Nabby a horrified look. "Oh, Nabby, pray forgive my careless tongue. I forgot that—"

"No matter," said Nabby. "Will will tell no tales, any more than he will reveal who else was there, lest the British take their revenge against all who—"

"What's this?" Nabby turned to see Master Butler, in heavy coat and cocked hat, standing in the doorway.

"Methinks, Nabby, you know a great deal about last night's events for a young maid presumed to be at home asleep." His voice turned cold. "Did I not give orders that none in this household were to cross the threshold last night?"

"Sir, those were your very words, repeated to us by Mistress Butler herself."

Master Butler turned as red as the wattles of a turkey cock. "Do you deny that you were at Griffin's Wharf last night?"

Nabby put on her meekest expression. "Oh, no, sir. I was there. Pray do not think me pert, but I did not cross the threshold. I climbed down the tree beside our window."

5

"*Smartly, boy!*" *Master Butler roared in the* workroom. "A snail that advances an inch an hour could easily outrun you nowadays. The fire not mended, the floor not swept, the—"

Nabby eased the kitchen door open a little farther, the better to hear what was going on, but she need not have done so. For once, Lonzo's voice, which was usually barely audible, rose high and angry.

"Treat me like dirt under your feet, will you?" he yelled. "You'll sing a different tune when I tell the British the name of one of the 'Indians' who dumped the tea into Boston Harbor!"

Nabby looked at Emily with horror. The British were indeed anxious to learn the names of the tea party men. Although half of Boston knew who they were, only one had been reported to the authorities and he only because he talked too much in the hearing of a spiteful neighbor. Will Truax doubted that there was a magistrate in Boston who would convict any of the patriots, but that might not prevent the British from trying, especially with Governor Hutchinson declaiming about high treason day and night.

"How came you to know who was there if you were not there yourself after I had ordered you to your room?" Master Butler's voice was hoarse with anger.

"The girl was there, too," said Lonzo. "Why is it worse for me than for her?"

"That tale-teller!" Nabby muttered to Emily. "And to think I kept his secret in spite of being found out myself!"

Luckily, Nabby's quick answer to Master Butler about not setting foot over the threshold had so diverted him that he had gone stamping back to his work without another word—a narrow escape indeed. Nabby had taken care to be a model of good behavior ever since. Now she listened for Master Butler's reply to the impertinent Lonzo.

"It is worse for you than for Nabby because, besides being disobedient, you threaten to betray your master." Master Butler bit off the words. "Have you forgotten the articles of your indenture, that you shall 'the master's lawful commands gladly everywhere obey, his secrets keep'? I would be within my rights to turn you out into the street."

"Do so, then!" Lonzo was defiant. "I have a bit put by, and the British will pay me well for—"

"Confound the British!" Master Butler raged. "And tell me, pray, where you got this 'bit' that you say you have put by?"

Nabby's attention was distracted from the quarrel in the workroom by the arrival at the shop door of a red-faced lady in a plumed bonnet and a little maidservant scurrying behind with a teapot in her hand.

"How may we serve you?" Mistress Butler curtsied

as she always did at sight of the gentry. "Your teapot is in need of repair, mayhap?"

"The finest bohea!" The lady shook the teapot under Mistress Butler's nose. "Why, 'tis not even tea, but some weed, I vow! And the boy swore it was rescued from the tea ships!"

"Boy? What boy?" Mistress Butler was completely bewildered. "Indeed, there must be some mistake."

"A mistake or worse. Pray summon this boy—your apprentice, according to Susan here"—she gestured toward the maidservant—"and I will teach him to make mistakes!"

"Nabby!" Nabby popped out from her listening post behind the kitchen door like a jack-in-the-box. "Pray fetch Master Butler at once!"

"Hand me down the pewter mug from that shelf yonder," the lady told Mistress Butler, "and I will pour you out a cup of this gruesome brew!"

"My husband will not allow a drop of British tea to touch my lips," Mistress Butler protested, but when Nabby returned with Master Butler, his wife, with a wry face, was sipping gingerly from the mug.

"Tea it is not," she assured her husband, "but what it is, I do not know, though it has a flavor like parsley. Nabby, go in to Emily and close the door behind you."

"As you say, ma'am," Nabby said demurely.

Stifling laughter, she again joined Emily in the kitchen. Although they listened with all their might, they could hear naught through the stout oak door save the rumble of Master Butler's voice, then a shout of "Lonzo!", then more talk, the slamming of doors, and silence. Mistress Butler, breathless, came hurrying in. "What a to-do!" she said. "Lonzo sold a packet of dried parsley, mayhap taken from my stores in the rafters, to an official's lady as tea from the *Dartmouth.* Tobias made him return the money he charged milady and has locked him in his room to meditate on his sins, with a touch of the switch to remind him."

"Nabby!" Master Butler would have made an excellent town crier, audible halfway to Long Wharf. "I have need of you!" She scurried fearfully to the workroom, to find Master Butler critically inspecting what appeared to be the newly cast lid for a teapot. "I will not ask you whether you played any part in this business of the parsley, but—"

"Then, sir, if you do not ask me, I need not answer," Nabby said cheerfully.

"And that will be a great saving of words. Whatever the facts, I cannot but chuckle at the thought of her ladyship serving dried parsley at her hoity-toity tea party. I have no doubt, however, that the packet originally contained tea, which by some means was transformed into parsley—a bit of magic that is too clever by far for Lonzo."

"Yes, sir," Nabby murmured.

"I see you will not be drawn, young Nabby. Very well. You shall pay for your tricks, whatever they are, by turning the lathe for me while Lonzo is considering whether to mend his ways."

"Oh, thank you, sir!" Nabby reached for the handle of the big wheel that kept the lathe turning, but Master Butler lifted a warning hand. "Make haste slowly, girl. There is more to this than turning a wheel with the speed of the wind. Pay heed now so you will know how to proceed next time."

Next time? Nabby clung to the words, which offered hope for the future.

"Very well," Master Butler went on. "First we must fasten the piece of pewter firmly to the lathe."

"How?" asked Nabby. "How do you fasten it?"

"Sometimes between centers, which are rods that clasp the work from either side, and other times by attaching the object to a chuck, but this you will hardly understand."

"No, sir, not yet, but I will, under your guidance."

"Mayhap." Master Butler refused to commit himself. "Pray hand me a burnisher from the shelf."

Bewildered, Nabby looked at an assortment of tools in various shapes.

"This one?" She chose at random, handing him a pointed tool shaped rather like the ace of spades.

"Nay. The round-headed one for now, although I may use several ere I finish. Your stint at the wheel begins as soon as I have this lid securely in place. You turn the wheel with the handle, the wheel turns the belt, the belt turns the lathe and the piece of pewter fastened to it. I steady the tool against this rail of wood so that it burnishes the pewter as it rotates with the lathe."

"Yes, sir." That seemed clear enough, but Nabby was not sure how long it would stay so.

"Very well. To the task."

There was a half-smile on his face, as though he doubted that Nabby was strong enough to turn the great wheel. For the first few moments, she could al-

most sympathize with Lonzo, for she was red-faced and puffing before she got the wheel well started. The task grew easier as the momentum of the wheel eased her work. At last, after Master Butler had changed from one tool to another two or three times, he pronounced himself satisfied. He held out the lid for Nabby to see.

"Smooth as satin now." He ran a hand over the glowing surface. "It takes time and patience to achieve such a sheen. Here is the teapot to which the lid will be attached. It, too, must be burnished, and, as you see, it still lacks a handle. What think you of a wooden ear-shaped one?"

"That will be fair indeed," said Nabby, "almost a match for the one in which you sent the message"—her voice faded but not in time to keep the words from coming out—"to the printer."

"Message?" Master Butler heaved an exasperated sigh. "It appears that you and Lonzo between you know as much about my business as I do."

"The difference is that I do not intend to let a word of it escape my lips. And pray do not link me with Lonzo, who mislikes me as much as I do him."

"Be that as it may, there must be a stop to all this snooping and prying."

"Oh, sir, my finding the paper was an accident— almost. The wrapping of the teapot started to come awry, and I stopped to rewrap it. Then I could not resist undoing it further to admire the beautiful sheen of the pewter."

"A good piece of work, English-made," Master Butler admitted.

"And then I heard a rustle within and—"

"And I suppose you read what was on the paper?"

"Nay, sir, I did not, although I fear I would have done so had I not been prevented by two women who thought it strange to find me kneeling beside a hedge with a pewter teapot in my hand." Nabby put on her most righteous look. "Afterward, though, I did my errand as you directed and came straight home."

Master Butler held his head. "You were at fault for meddling, but you were right to tell me the truth, so the scales of justice seem to be in tolerable balance. Therefore, you will receive no punishment, nor any praise either."

"Yes, sir, and I thank you for your kindness." She could not resist what she hoped was a nudge in the right direction. "Tell me true, sir, did I turn the wheel as well as Lonzo? And may I help you again sometime?"

"Anyone with muscle can turn the wheel. The rest takes skill and a fondness for the work. As for replacing Lonzo, which I think is in your mind, I have my part of the agreement to fulfill, wearing though it is." He set his teeth. "But I will mold that boy as I would a piece of pewter if there is an ounce of sturdy metal in him to work with."

Nabby doubted that there was, but she could understand Master Butler's determination to finish what he had set out to do. She had exactly the same feeling about learning to make pewter.

"I must remind you," Master Butler went on, "that your first duty here is to Emily."

"Yes, sir, and if you have no further need of me, I shall go to her at once." She went with lagging steps to the door. "Emily would be happy to help you, too, or, if she cannot help, merely to sit and watch as she did a few days ago."

"How can a man work in a room crowded with people?" Master Butler demanded. "There is naught but talk,talk, talk where females are gathered."

Nabby sprang to Emily's defense. "I warrant that Emily uttered not a word that day when she sat drawing in a corner here. It is not her fault that she is not a boy."

Master Butler's face turned bleak. "True for you, it is not, but—" He struggled for words for a moment and then waved Nabby away. "Begone, girl. You speak of things you do not understand."

Nabby went soberly back to the kitchen. It was true that she had been remiss in her duty to Emily, for, although she had persuaded Will Truax to bring Emily spare sheets of paper whenever he had them, she had not yet found a way to take her charge abroad to see the sights of the town. For now, that might be just as well since the winter, which had started out mildly, turned severe during January.

"You promised to help me," Nabby told Will Truax one cold day when, bundled to the ears, she met him as she fared forth to market for Mistress Butler, sitting warm by the fire at home.

"I promised that I would think about it," Will argued.

"Think, then."

Will stamped his feet to keep them warm. "A sled would be easy," he finally said, "a mere matter of two barrel staves fastened to the legs of a chair, which a sturdy girl like you could easily push."

Being thought of as a sturdy girl was of no great interest to Nabby, except in the case of Master Butler, who must be convinced that she was physically equal to the task of pewtering.

"A sled!" she sputtered. "Spring will be coming soon—at least it always has—and we must be making our plans."

"Leave off, Nabby! I think better when a cold wind is not whistling around my ears." He sobered. "Do not think me unmindful of Emily's plight. My master leaves me little time for myself but sends me forth to listen and watch and so learn the temper of the people. He fears what will happen when news of the Boston Tea Party reaches London."

"Which may already have happened," said Nabby, "if the winds have been fair. Did not the *Hayley* sail for England just before Christmas with a witness or two aboard?"

"Aye, and with letters from Sam Adams and Dr. Warren to the Massachusetts agent in London. The *Dartmouth* followed a fortnight or so later."

In the meantime, Boston was boiling with talk. Should the town pay for the destroyed tea to avoid further trouble with Britain? Most patriots were defiantly opposed to that. Paul Revere, whom Sam Adams had dispatched to New York and Philadelphia the day after the tea was thrown into the harbor, had ridden home again soon after Christmas to report that cheers and the ringing of church bells had greeted his news. The Widow Parsons, on one of Nabby's hasty visits, vowed that the fish caught in the harbor had a strange taste from the tea in which they had been swimming and that therefore it might be both unpatriotic and unhealthy to eat them.

"And if the British learn that they taste of bohea," she added, "they may try to tax them on that account."

Emily sat cheerfully by the fire drawing pictures of the tea party from Nabby's description—disguised men swarming over the ships, tea showering into the water, the watching crowd, the flaring torches. For someone who never left the house, Emily had caught the spirt of the occasion remarkably well.

"Thanks to you!" she told Nabby, who had corrected the outline of a ship now and then or remembered a detail or two.

Emily had also finished the sketch of her father's workroom, which Nabby showed him when Emily was too shy to do so.

"What have we here?" He spread it out on the table on which the family had just eaten a supper of fish and corn pudding. He pulled a newly made candlestick closer. "The wheel, the forge, the lathe, even some of the tools." He looked at his daughter with some surprise. "You have a sharp eye. But who is this turning the wheel—not Lonzo surely, in skirts and a white cap?"

" 'Tis Nabby, Father," Emily ventured. "Did she not turn the wheel for you one day?"

"Aye, she did, in Lonzo's place." He studied the sketch a moment longer. "And what do I see in the corner? A mouse? Must I tell your mother to bait a trap?"

"The mouse," said Nabby, "represents Emily herself. Did she not promise to sit in the corner as quiet as a mouse?"

Master Butler's face was expressionless. "Next time, Emily, pray draw yourself as you are. I do not fancy a mouse for a daughter, though 'tis an ingenious fancy."

A pathetic one, in Nabby's opinion, for who had turned Emily into a mouse except her busy, troubled father?

Lonzo, as always, had eaten in sullen silence and betaken himself to his room. A little later, since his work was done for the day, he would go forth with other apprentices to roister through the streets, throw snowballs at British soldiers in from Castle William, and make whatever mischief they could without arousing the watch. Nabby knew the ways of apprentices, at least some of them, from her days in the hurly-burly of Long Wharf.

From the absence of shouting in the workroom nowadays, Nabby judged that Lonzo had not given further trouble. He might not care about pewtering, but presumably he did care about eating. He spoke to Nabby only once, when he encountered her at the kitchen door.

"You did it!" he snarled. "You put that parsley in the tea packet!"

"And threw the traitorous tea away, too," Nabby agreed, "but I did not tell Master Butler about it. I am not a teller of tales, like others within a stone's throw of me."

Lonzo muttered something unintelligible and

lumbered off to the workroom shaking his head as though a swarm of gnats were buzzing around his ears.

Nabby was not invited again to help Master Butler. She hoped it was because he now had Lonzo under control and not because her work had been unsatisfactory. From a kitchen that smelled of a long winter's cooking, she looked wearily at the cold streets and longed for spring. Then the doors would stand open to let in the scent of green things, mingled with the familiar odor of tar, spices, tobacco, fish, and salty sea air from the wharves along the waterfront.

She tried to think less about spring and the wharves and more about transportation for Emily. Will Truax had suggested a chair on runners, so why not a chair on wheels? Nabby had once seen a man riding out comfortably, though not very fashionably, in a chair mounted on a pair of wheels and drawn by a horse. Something of the sort, on smaller wheels so Nabby could push it, might do nicely—if she had the chair and if she had the wheels. She hoped she could think of something less conspicuous than a household chair, for Emily might feel shy of being stared at like a two-headed calf as Nabby propelled her through the streets of Boston. Mayhap this was all a dream since Nabby had no way of buying what she needed, even if she knew exactly what it was. Still, if she kept her eyes open and nagged Will Truax into doing the same, something might occur to her.

"Wheels?" said the Widow Parsons when Nabby told her about her plans for Emily one bitter day when she had squeezed out a few moments from her errands to visit Long Wharf. "There are wheels everywhere."

She looked out at a wharf bustling with wagons, carts, and barrows.

"And none the right size, even if they were mine," said Nabby.

"You have money to pay?"

"Nay, I do not, though—" Her thoughts shied away from her porringer, which it would break her heart to sell.

The Widow Parsons looked at her downcast face. "Take heart, Nabby. 'Tis always darkest before the dawn. I will speak to some of my tobacco customers. Men are ever eager to give advice to poor helpless women."

With a nod of thanks, Nabby hurried out as two grizzled sailors came in. She looked longingly at a ship or two unloading just opposite where her mother's shop used to be. It was now occupied by a counting house, where Nabby glimpsed clerks perched on high stools poring over thick ledgers. The windows in the little rooms abovestairs that she and her mother—and her father too, between voyages—had occupied stared dustily out over the harbor, pewter-colored under wintry clouds. She hesitated. She wanted to walk up to the pewterer's on Back Street to peer through the window and see whether he had any bigger stock of finished goods than Master Butler, but she decided against that as it would make her late home, and if Mistress Butler was too sorely tried, she would run her errands herself —or so she said.

"Though there is nobody like you for picking up bits of gossip," Mistress Butler had once declared, "and who would mind the shop if I were gone?"

"I tended shop for my mother all day long many a time," Nabby had said with a spark of fire in her voice, "so if worse comes to worst—"

Now she spared one last moment to admire a square-rigger approaching Bird Island. It was just the kind of ship she intended to use as her touchmark if the day came when she had one. She took a second look. Then she ran for home—King to Kilby, Kilby to Milk—and burst without ceremony into Master Butler's workroom.

"She is here at last!" Nabby panted. "The *Boston Traveller*!"

"At least one tea ship brought us a welcome cargo, though long enough delayed." Will Truax elbowed his way to Nabby through a cluster of people following a lamplighter in heavy coat, breeches, and gaiters putting flame for the first time to Boston's new streetlamps. "My master says the town will see things clearer now, in more ways than one."

Nabby, fascinated by the flare of light along a street often darker than the inside of a boot, nodded absently. The three-hundred-odd iron streetlamps had been salvaged from the fourth tea ship, the brig *William,* driven aground on Cape Cod at the time of the tea party. The tea chests had been saved, too, to the patriots' disgust, and were now stored at Castle William under British care. The lamplighter touched off another wick, and a pool of light glittered on the icy street. Nabby took care to note the look of the lamps and their posts so she could describe them well to Emily.

"Ah, there, Nabby!" Silas Bridges, with the Widow Parsons on his arm, hailed her. "Master Butler has told you that all went well with our little piece of business?" Master Butler had not, exactly, but the increased supply of tin in the workroom the last few weeks spoke for itself. "We will hope to bring another supply on the next trip." He glanced at Will. "Is it not the printer's apprentice?"

"It is," said Will. "Out to see Boston all alight."

"Aye, a fair sight," said Silas, "which I shall think on when I am buffeted by wind, wave, and darkness on my way to England."

"You will sail soon?" asked Nabby, who had been wondering why the *Boston Traveller* had not departed long since.

"Tomorrow, with the first tide. We have a cargo after a month's wait and are hoping for a fair wind." He shook his head. "The second day of March, and winter still upon us!"

"I have been telling Silas of your need for wheels, Nabby," the Widow Parsons said.

"Were it sails or barrels of rum or salt air, I could help you," said Silas, "but wheels have naught to do with the sea, though the *Traveller* sometimes rolls as though it were some wheeled conveyance of the devil himself." He glanced at her thoughtfully. "You have the look of your father about you, girl, and his ways, too, methinks. He was ever one to contrive ingenious ways of doing things."

Nabby did not think she was ingenious at all, else she would have found a means by now for Emily to move about the town.

"Wheels?" Will Truax gave Nabby a puzzled look, then a guilty one. "Oh, for Emily's transport."

"Certainly for Emily's transport," said Nabby. "I

venture you have not given it a thought. Not only that, she is in need of more paper for her drawings."

"I do have a sheet or two, smudged from the press," said Will. "We are printing few broadsides these days, for who would stop in a chill east wind to read a handbill tacked to a tree? Besides, that same wind would whirl it away in no time."

The east wind was doing its worst now. Nabby pulled her cloak closer around her.

"I must bid you all good evening," she said, "since I am expected at home. A safe voyage to you, Silas Bridges, and a safe return as well."

"I will see you to your door," said Will. "I would not have thought your mistress would allow you from home in the darkness."

" 'Tis not as dark as it was before the new lamps," said Nabby, astonished at his solicitude, "but I will thank you for your company."

"Pray tell Emily I will bring her the paper as soon as may be," said Will, "and I will inquire about wheels."

"And about something to put them on, too," said Nabby, "and a way to pay as well."

"Is that all?" he demanded. "Would you not also like me to think of the means to free us from the heavy hand of Britain? In my spare moments, of course."

Nabby sobered. For all the show of good cheer under the new streetlamps, all Boston knew that the town would not go unpunished for the tea party.

"I have no doubt that at this very moment there is a great to-do in Parliament on the subject," Master Butler had said gloomily.

In spite of his forebodings, he was in better temper since Silas Bridges and his shipmates on the *Boston Traveller* had brought him his few bars of tin. He even allowed Nabby in the workroom to watch whenever Emily did not need her. Indeed, he was almost genial on the morning after the lighting of the streetlamps.

"Listen carefully!" He snapped the edge of a pewter basin with his middle finger. "Hear the ring?" Next, he flicked an old plate that he was preparing to melt down. "Dull, is it not? Pewter that is mostly tin like the basin has a resonance to it as well as a beautiful sheen, but that made with, say, twenty percent lead sounds dull to match its muddy look. Take heed again."

He snapped the basin and the plate in turn— bright to dull in sound and appearance. Lonzo stood by, elaborately uninterested. Although Master Butler was talking in his direction, Nabby knew that the words were meant for her as much as for Lonzo.

"With the new tin, I am able, for a while at least, to make pewter of which I can be proud."

That was a backhanded way of thanking her for her part in the project without letting the treacherous Lonzo know where the tin had come from. It still seemed unfair that Master Butler had not taken her as an apprentice after she had introduced him to Silas Bridges as a possible source of tin that first day. Despite all, however, she was learning a little about pewter, for her own satisfaction even if naught else ever came of it.

"Nabby!" Master Butler called her thoughts back to the matter at hand. "Never did I think you would be woolgathering while I was talking about pewter. Pray repeat what I just said."

"You said—" She sighed. Thinking about her own disappointment, she had let valuable information slip past her. "You said that with the new tin you can make pewter that rings like a bell and shines like silver."

"Did I, now? That was three sentences back. Besides, such poetical words are as much like me as a satin slipper is like a stout buckled shoe. Still— You, Lonzo, what did I say?"

"You said a satin slipper is not like a buckled shoe," Lonzo mumbled.

Master Butler threw up his hands. "Before that, boy! When Nabby was not listening."

Lonzo shook his head.

"Take note, then, both of you." Master Butler spoke slowly and distinctly. "I said that copper and antimony added to the tin harden and strengthen the alloy and give it that resonance we were admiring."

"My porringer is a good alloy, is it not?" Nabby asked.

Lonzo turned aside, muttering, "That porringer! If I never heard tell of it again, it would be too soon. You would think there was not another porringer in all of Boston."

"And so there is not, for me!" Nabby flared. "Indeed, you would not know good pewter from bad, or care either!"

"Enough!" Master Butler's patience was obviously wearing thin. "Lonzo, no more ill words to Nabby, and, Nabby, a sharp tongue gains naught."

"Yes, sir," said Nabby, "and I ask your pardon for my inattention earlier. It was not from lack of interest but only that I have plans afoot."

"As do we all," Master Butler said wearily. "You may return to Emily now. Lonzo, as is his duty, will turn the wheel while I put the final polish on yonder beaker."

Back in the kitchen, Nabby found Emily moping beside the fire. Even had she had paper to draw on, she had nothing to draw except from her imagination and from Nabby's description of the lamplighting. Nothing stirred in the wintry scene outside the window except one small gray bird to whom Nabby had thrown a few crumbs when Mistress Butler was safely out of sight in the shop. Mistress Butler would not have begrudged the crumbs since Nabby had kept them back from her own piece of corn cake, but she would have minded Nabby's opening the kitchen door even a crack to toss out the crumbs and lose heat from a room already none too warm. Even close to the fire, Emily was shivering a little.

"Roasted on the front, frozen on the back," Nabby said. "It was ever thus in winter. What you need is a barrel chair, like the one my father made me, to keep the drafts away from the side and rear and—"

She stopped, with her mouth open like a fish gasping on shore. Of course! A barrel chair was what Emily must have atop those wheels whenever Nabby got them. The next chance she had, she would walk past the cooper's, just in case he might have a faulty barrel he would part with for— For nothing, which was all Nabby had. Still, looking was cheap and sometimes led to unexpected things. The cooper's child, if he had one, might toddle into the street and Nabby would dart out and snatch it from under the wheels of a passing carriage. The grateful cooper would give her a free barrel, and the owner of the carriage, impressed by her alertness, might offer a cash reward. Nabby sighed at her own foolishness.

"When dreaming, Emily," she said, "as well dream of silver and gold as of wood and stone. It costs no more and is much more pleasant while it lasts."

"Nabby!" Master Butler summoned her into the workroom. "You know the pewterer on Back Street? I must needs send you to return this candlestick mold I borrowed from him. I mislike using another's mold, but, expensive as they are, few of us have a choice. Pray give him my thanks and ask for the return of my ladle mold since I have an order to fill. No need for haste; 'tis a long walk."

No walk was too long for Nabby, always happy to be out and away. As for haste, if she hurried part of the way, she would have leisure later to peer into the cooper's and also the print shop, on the chance of collecting the paper Will Truax had promised. She walked sedately up Milk Street until she was out of sight of the Butlers and then scurried to Marlborough, turning to pass the Old South Meeting House, as quiet now as though no "Indians" had ever burst forth from the town meeting to throw the tea into Boston Harbor. Cornhill took her across King, down which she could glimpse Long Wharf, with several ships unloading alongside. She hesitated, drawn, as though by a magnet, to her old haunts.

"With your love of the sea and ships, you would have made a good seaman," her father had once said, "had you only been born a boy."

Everything interesting, it seemed, was reserved for men and boys, even pewtering, which overshadowed both the sea and ships in Nabby's mind. Why should it matter whether one was a boy or a girl? Nabby had turned the lathe as well as Lonzo, and she understood far more about the whole pewtering process than he did, for all the time he had spent under Master Butler's teaching. She kicked angrily at a still-frozen lump of snow, which flew down the street and bounced off the shin of a British soldier who was rounding the corner from the State House.

"Forgive me." Nabby gave him a cold stare. "I was not aiming at you."

The redcoat looked pointedly down the empty street. "Who were you aiming at, then?" He rubbed his shin. "I would as soon meet a squadron of wildcats as one rebellious colonial." He scowled. "But since we are forbidden to stir up the natives further, pray pass on, your ladyship."

Nabby swished by with her nose in the air. At the last moment, the soldier thrust out a foot to trip her, but she leaped lightly over and, laughing, turned into Dock Square and down to the print shop. Here was an adventure to describe to Emily. Indeed, nearly every time Nabby fared forth she met with an adventure of some kind. Mayhap it was because she never bothered to put on ladylike manners—the downcast look (how would she see what was going on?) and the timid air (no help at elbowing her way through crowds). For all her courageous manner, she was glad to see Will Truax just outside the print shop. Quiet as Boston seemed at the moment, anger between the British and the rebel Bostonians simmered under the surface, ready to break out at any moment.

"A British soldier tried to trip me," Nabby announced. "He thought I threw a chunk of frozen snow at him."

"And did you?"

"I merely kicked it," said Nabby, "for reasons of my own."

"Fair enough." Will swayed as though his foot had slipped on the ice. "Where are you bound for?"

"To the pewterer's on Back Street. Also—"

Will, turning white, leaned abruptly against the print shop wall.

"You are ill," Nabby cried anxiously. "Shall I bring help?"

Will managed a wan smile. "I am beyond help, thanks to that ferry to Charlestown, where I had to go to deliver some printing. It rocked and tossed until—"

"You had best hasten to lie down in your room, and I will tell your master so."

"No, no! I would be ashamed to admit that I cannot set foot on a boat of any kind without—"

He vanished abruptly through the back door of the print shop. Nabby shrugged. So there would be no paper for Emily today, all because of the Charlestown ferry. Nabby hurried on to Back Street and halted in front of a shop with a sign shaped like a teapot. The pewterer was standing in the doorway.

"Master Butler returns your candlestick mold, with thanks," said Nabby, "and begs his ladle mold back."

The pewterer beckoned her inside. While he searched for the ladle mold, she stood admiring his stock of pewterware, displayed on shelves as in Master Butler's shop. Her attention was drawn especially to a teapot delicately banded with an etched design of flowers and leaves.

"That, sir, is a handsome piece of work." Nabby was fishing for information, since she would not for the world admit that Master Butler had nothing of the kind in his shop.

"And here is another." The pewterer brought out a warming pan, decorated over its entire top with a pattern of sprays and flowers. "Wriggled work."

"Requiring great skill," said Nabby as though she knew all about it.

"Not so much—engraving of a simple type." The pewterer picked up a small flat tool. "Held at an angle, so, and pushed with a rocking or wriggling motion, it makes pretty little designs. It is a matter of practice, like all else in this craft, lest the pattern be too deeply cut and weaken the pewter to the cracking point."

He was just like Master Butler, ever eager to talk about his work and its problems. With ladle mold in hand, Nabby headed for home, hurrying again because of all the time she had spent talking and listening. Will Truax, apparently recovered after a few more minutes on dry land, darted from the back door of the print shop, handed Nabby a few sheets of paper, and rushed back inside before Nabby could do more than call

"Thank you" after him. At home, she hurried into Master Butler's workroom with the ladle mold.

"My thanks," he said abstractedly, pouring molten metal into a plate mold. "Have you seen or heard aught of note?"

"Will Truax sent some paper for Emily's drawings, and I saw some wriggled work at the pewterer's —new to me, although I did not say so."

"And I venture you found out all about it," said Master Butler. "I have no skill in that direction myself nor much taste for it either. Plain pewter with honest lines and a bit of beading is more my style, although the ladies might sometimes fancy more elaborate decoration. I even have a tool for the purpose somewhere here. Look on the middle shelf alongside the large burnisher."

"May I borrow it for study?" asked Nabby. "I am eager to learn the tools of the trade."

"Take note of her interest, Lonzo," Master Butler said. "You may well profit from her example."

"Oh, sir," said Nabby in a deceptively humble voice, "I am only a girl and therefore incapable of being an example to anyone."

She wished the words unspoken the moment they were out of her mouth. Master Butler would recognize them as unseemly sarcasm, uttered in a flare of temper that had taken even Nabby by surprise.

"Again I ask your pardon," Nabby said, scarlet-faced. "That was ill-spoken indeed."

Lonzo, as expected, took her remark at face value.

"But you *are* a girl," he said with a curl of the lip, "and so not to be—"

"Silence!" Master Butler roared. "The making of good pewter is trial enough without an endless battle of words." His voice deepened. "I will have no more of it."

"It was Nabby who—" Lonzo began, but at sight of Master Butler's thunderous face he gulped down whatever words he had been about to utter.

Nabby scuttled out, thoroughly discouraged with herself. Twice in one day she had fallen into disfavor with Master Butler, all because she had not curbed her tongue or her thoughts, or tried very hard either. That must change at once or all her dreams would go glimmering, if they had not already. With an effort she put on a cheerful face for Emily.

"Look!" she cried. "I have brought you paper from Will Truax, who is seasick from the Charlestown ferry, poor lad. Not only that—"

It was on the tip of her tongue to speak of the barrel chair, but she decided it was best to wait until she saw a way to reach her goal. Instead, she produced the unnamed tool that Master Butler had given her. At that moment a whole cluster of ideas flashed across her mind with the brilliance of the lightning that Benjamin Franklin, the noted scientist, was said to have tamed with a metal rod thrust into the ground.

"This," said she, "will be the means of—of changing your whole life."

"Wriggled work!" Emily said gleefully. "Does this make me a wriggler, kin to a worm or a pollywog?"

She and Nabby had hurried to their bedchamber early to practice in private on the old pewter plate that Nabby had managed to purloin from Master Butler's scrap-metal box. Candlelight flickered on Emily's intent face.

"The design is easy enough." She consulted a simple pattern of leaves and berries that she had drawn on a scrap of paper. "But the rest is not so—"

The tool slipped, and the plate, which Nabby was doing her best to steady, flew out of her hands and skidded across the table, sending her precious porringer clanging to the floor.

"Oh!" Emily's hands flew to her mouth as Nabby dived under the table. "I would not for the world have done aught to harm the porringer."

"Neither dent nor nick," Nabby said cheerfully.

There was a small mark where the porringer had hit the floor, but she would not dream of mentioning it. The plate had a deep scratch across its face—no matter, since it was destined to be melted down later and become a brave new piece of pewter.

"Your father's vise would be useful," said Nabby. "Mayhap it is a mistake to keep this all a secret until you grow more skillful, but I need time to complete my plans."

"And I the same to learn," said Emily, "but I can do it. I know I can."

"Of course you can. Your father will be the only pewterer in Boston with his own artist doing wriggled work to order."

Master Butler did not yet know of his good fortune. Neither did Nabby know where she was going to get more old pewter for Emily to practice on, for Master Butler would be sure to notice if his scanty store of scrap metal kept diminishing. It was all very well to say blithely that the wriggling would change Emily's whole life, but it would take a deal of scheming to make it so.

Nabby steadied the plate again for Emily and gloomily counted the problems that might thwart her ambitious project. Emily might not be strong enough to score the metal. Even though she were and could learn the art, Master Butler might not allow her to decorate his precious pewter. Nabby tended to agree with him that pewter was best when it depended on beauty of line and remained almost entirely unadorned, but even Master Butler admitted that every customer did not have the same taste. Besides, if Master Butler could not be persuaded to use Emily's talents, there were other pewterers in Boston—a daring thought.

"There!" Emily put down the tool and eased her cramped fingers. "Only one small cluster of berries"—she looked at it critically—"and that somewhat lopsided."

"Only because the plate kept slipping." Nabby rubbed Emily's hands. "You do not find the work too tiring?"

"Oh, no!" She gave Nabby a twisted smile. "My hands and shoulders have grown strong from hauling myself about the house on my crutches—one small return for my sorry plight, the only one except that it brought you here to—to do kind things for me."

"A lucky day for me as well," said Nabby, touched, "when I became a member of your household."

It had been pewter and not Emily that had brought her here, but Emily's need had given her the chance to stay. If she could manage to keep in Master Butler's good graces, she hoped to do great things for Emily, even though not for herself—yet. She still stubbornly refused to accept the possibility that her dream of becoming a pewterer's apprentice might always remain merely a dream.

Bent on putting her plans in motion at once, she stopped at the cooper's the next morning on her way to market—a chore that Mistress Butler, now convinced of her bargaining powers, had turned over to her entirely.

"I am in search of a barrel," she told the cooper. "A flawed one would do, since it is for a chair, but it must be unused."

Emily, she felt sure, would not fancy riding around

Boston in a barrel that smelled of tobacco, salt fish, molasses, or rum.

"A chair?" The cooper stopped his work to stare at her. "A chair made out of a barrel?"

"Yes, sir." Nabby explained the way of making it as best she could. "I do not have money to pay at the moment, but if you should chance to come upon a suitable barrel, I would thank you for saving it for me until I can find the money."

"That I will," said the cooper, "if I do not decide to make a few chairs of my own in odd moments."

"Surely, in that case, you would owe me a barrel for suggesting a use for your damaged ones," Nabby said brightly. "My name is Abigail Jonas, and I may be reached at Master Butler's, where I am indentured. The chair will be for his daughter Emily, who is in my care."

"Say you so? And does not Master Butler have chairs in plenty?"

"Not for this purpose. I plan to attach wheels to the barrel chair so that I may take Emily forth to see the sights." Then, at his puzzled look: "She is crippled, sir, from the distemper of a few years ago and has barely set foot over the threshold since."

"To be sure. I had forgotten, although my good wife told me of it. Did not Master Butler lose a son at that time, too?"

"He did," Nabby said shortly, "but it is fortunate he has a daughter left, for she has a talent of her own." As the shadow of an entering customer fell across the door, Nabby added hastily, "Master Butler knows naught of this, for he must work from dawn to dusk at the pewtering which puts the bread in our mouths."

"So it is with all of us." The cooper gave Nabby a long look. "You are Seaman Jonas's daughter, mayhap?" Nabby nodded. "A good man. We were boys together. Have no fear. I will find you a barrel, soon or late." He nodded to the customer. "Sir?"

So far, so good. True, Nabby did not yet have the barrel or the wheels or, worse, the means to pay for them, but at least the cooper knew her wants and might spread the word among the artisans of the town. Even with the barrel and the wheels, she would need someone to build the chair. She must consult Will Truax about that as well as about finances.

Her mind turned on her porringer, which might pay for Emily's transport if there were no other way. People, she told herself firmly, were more important than objects, even as dear a possession as the porringer.

In the days that followed, Emily toiled at her wriggled work and Nabby fretted. It was a time for waiting—for Emily to grow proficient in wriggling, for the cooper to send word that he had a suitable barrel for her, and for Will Truax, who, for all Nabby knew, had been laid low by another trip on the Charlestown ferry, to offer suggestions about the wheels. Indeed, all Boston seemed to be waiting, amid meetings both public and private, for news—almost certain to be bad—of how England had reacted to the tea party. It was April by the calendar, but a chilly rain poured down, slicking the cobblestones and making puddles for Nabby to leap, with skirts held a shade higher than Mistress Butler might think proper.

On such a day, with her market basket well covered lest the fish inside, thinking it had returned to the sea, should revive and try to swim away, Nabby paused at the Widow Parsons' for a bit of gossip. With her elbows on the counter and a candle for light, the widow was laboriously spelling out the news in a damp copy of the *Gazette*.

"Read it for me, Nabby!" Her fingers rested on a small notice in one corner of the front page. " 'Tis something for sale, but the print is so fine and the day so dark that I had as soon try to read at the bottom of a well." She smiled. "Besides, I was ever slow with my letters."

"For sale," Nabby read, "on Lime Street, near Charter, the household effects of the late Sara Hawkins, widow of Seaman Hawkins: Chairs, a settle, two bedsteads, a coverlet, an iron pot, treenware, pewter."

Nabby read no farther but bolted out of the tobacco shop toward home with only a wave of the hand for the Widow Parsons.

"A plate or a spoon or two would be all that a seaman's widow would have, methinks," said Master Butler when Nabby told him about the pewter.

"True for you." Nabby bit off the words. "And that little being sold for funeral expenses, no doubt, as were my mother's few bits and pieces."

Master Butler stared at Nabby's stormy face.

"Be not too quick to take offense," he said. "In this world some have more, and some have less, and no disgrace on either side. Go then and buy what pewter you judge usable with the few coins I can spare. Pewter for remelting is worth, at the most, ten pence a pound. A quart pot in good condition might go for three and six, and all else accordingly. Remember to pay heed more to the quality of the metal than to the nicks and dents." He dropped a bit of money into her hand as Lonzo looked on hungrily. "There is not enough there for you to go far astray, and my wife says you are a good bargainer." Then, without a change of expression: "For treenware, bid nothing at all. We have that and to spare in our kitchen, as I am often reminded."

The family, in spite of all the pewter in the house, ate mostly from wooden trenchers—treenware because they were made from trees—with Mistress Butler sometimes muttering darkly about shoemakers' children having no shoes. The few pewter plates and bowls were kept for guests, of whom the Butlers had had none since Nabby's arrival. One of the bowls was secretly abovestairs even now being adorned with wriggled work by the tireless Emily.

Nabby rushed off to the Hawkins house, arriving just in time to snatch two battered plates and a small basin from under the nose of a bearded peddler about to set forth on his westward tour. Nabby recognized him as one of the men who always awaited the seamen from the *Boston Traveller*.

"You again!" he muttered. "We had all thought ourselves well rid of you."

"Never count on such good fortune," said Nabby. "Like the flowers, I spring up everywhere." She spared him a smile. "My master would be glad to buy any damaged pewter that you might pick up in your travels—if the price were right."

She knew that many peddlers could mend broken spoons and bent plates in a crude way, well enough for the far frontier but not up to Master Butler's standards.

"Or," she went on, "he might make new pewterware by melting down what you bring him and adding other metals. You could sell that on next year's trip."

"Could I, indeed? Have you taken over your master's business while also telling me how to run mine?"

Nabby shrugged. "Have it your own way. A bit of profit here and another there adds up—for you as well as for Master Butler. I daresay the more sharp-witted peddlers will recognize a good deal when they see one."

She flounced off with the pewter in her basket, leaving the peddler standing indecisively. He caught up with her just as she was turning the corner.

"Did I not have to shoulder my pack and make a good start before nightfall, I would speak with your master now. Tell him on my account that I will watch for pewter and try to come to some agreement with him when I return in the autumn. My name is Jeremiah Curtin."

Nabby nodded. Now that she had stated so boldly what Master Butler would do, she was dubious. He was not a man who would appreciate a girl's speaking for him in matters of business or anything else. Still, Jeremiah Curtin would have been across Boston Neck into the countryside and the opportunity lost before she could fetch Master Butler to make his own arrangements. She would broach the subject later since Jeremiah Curtin would be gone all summer and might bring back no pewter in the fall anyway. For now,

Nabby must try to keep Master Butler in good humor for the unveiling of Emily's new talent since many things hung on his approval.

Master Butler was pleased with her purchases and the small price she paid—fortunately, since almost at once she needed his good will. The cooper sent a note, passed in at the kitchen door by his apprentice, that he was saving a proper barrel for her, the Widow Parsons had learned that the wheelwright had a pair of smallish wheels that might serve Nabby's purpose, and Mistress Butler, cleaning her cupboard from top to bottom in a fit of energy, discovered that her second-best pewter bowl was missing.

" 'Twill be that Lonzo!" she cried. "Indeed, I would not trust him from here to the doorstep. Did he not take the tea from—"

"Lonzo is not at fault," said Nabby. "I took the bowl."

"You?" Mistress Butler stared. "Never would I have thought— Tobias! Tobias! Come at once!"

Master Butler came hurrying out of his workroom with Lonzo at his heels.

"Nabby has—" Words failed Mistress Butler, and she sank down on the settle by the fire. "She has—"

Master Butler surveyed his distraught wife. "Speak, woman! What has Nabby done?" He suddenly remembered Lonzo, goggle-eyed behind him. "Return to the workroom, boy, and tidy my shelf of tools." Lonzo went, with a backward glance that told Nabby how glad he was to see her in disfavor. "And close the door," Master Butler called after him. "Now, what villainy has Nabby done?"

"I took Mistress Butler's second-best bowl be-cause—"

"Because I had need of it." Emily finally found her voice. "I had naught else left to practice my wriggled work on."

"Wriggled work!" Master Butler stood with his arms akimbo. "I might have known! Where is this bowl with the wriggled work on it?"

"Abovestairs," Emily quavered. "We have been working at night for a—a surprise."

"Go and fetch the bowl, Nabby," Master Butler ordered.

She scuttled up the stairs. She had planned to choose an evening when Master Butler, genial and well fed, was sitting in the kitchen with the smoke from his clay pipe curling upward. Then she would show him Emily's work when he was in a mood to ap-preciate it, not, as now, when the house was in such an uproar that he had been drawn away from his work. Upstairs, she tapped her porringer three times for luck and pulled the bowl with its wriggled band of flowers from its hiding place under Emily's bed. She rushed back downstairs—Master Butler was ever im-patient of being kept waiting—and handed him the bowl.

"Is it not nicely done?" she demanded. "Emily drew the design herself."

Master Butler turned the bowl critically from side to side.

"I see a flaw in one of the flowers," he said, "as though the tool had slipped."

"A flaw!" cried Nabby. "Pray recall that we had

no vise to hold it steady, but only my two hands." She drew a deep breath. "Sir, would you allow Emily to decorate some of your pewterware"—in spite of herself her voice shook a little—"and pay her a bit for her work? She could design whatever the customer would wish and—"

Her words were greeted by an astonished silence.

"Oh, but—" Emily began.

Nabby, who knew Emily was about to say that she would dearly love to work for her father for the pure pleasure of it, gestured her to silence.

"Pay her?" Master Butler said at last. "Where would I get the money to pay her?"

"From the extra you would get for your pewter if it were decorated to order," said Nabby.

"And what need has she for money? Is she not fed and clothed and—"

"And cut off from life," Nabby said passionately. "With only a little money I could provide transport for her—a chair on wheels that I could push about the town."

Now Emily was staring in astonishment, too.

"Oh, Nabby, could you indeed?"

"I could," said Nabby, "and I will." She made the final plunge. "I will sell my porringer if need be."

"No!" said Emily. "That you will not do if I"— tears filled her eyes—"if I never fare forth from this house all my life long." She turned to her father. "The porringer is Nabby's dearest treasure, and why should she do for me what my own parents will not?"

Master Butler looked from one girl to the other.

"Cannot, rather," he said slowly. "I—"

There was a great clatter at the kitchen door, and Will Truax backed in, dragging a fine new barrel and carrying a barrelhead under one arm.

"From the cooper," he said, "who saw me passing."

Nabby was close to tears herself. "But I cannot pay," she said, "until I sell my porringer."

"He says you owe him naught," said Will, "for he has made two chairs himself already from his damaged stock and has an order for yet another. As for the wheels, I have heard that—" He turned and saw Master Butler. "Your pardon, sir."

He pushed the barrel in Nabby's direction and left faster than he had come.

"What is this talk of barrels and wheels?" Master Butler demanded. "It seems I know naught of what goes on in my own house."

"We did not wish to interrupt your work." Nabby put on her most soothing tone. "Besides, you have told me time and again that I am here only to care for Emily—which is what I am doing."

"The barrel, girl."

"Yes, sir." Nabby looked admiringly at its pale wheaten color. "It is my plan for Emily to travel around Boston in the barrel, and—" Emily looked at her round-eyed, obviously alarmed at the thought of being rolled about in a barrel. "Made into a chair with wheels, silly! Not only that—"

At the end of her story, Master Butler sat in silence for a moment.

"Clever enough," he said finally, "save that I cannot spare money to pay for the wheels or to have the chair built out of this—this barrel. I am hard put to it to keep my shop stocked with metal nowadays, much less customers. Since the tea party, there are some here who could buy but are loath to patronize any they consider disloyal to the crown. Indeed, I have paid dearly for my part in that night's events. I regret nothing, save at times like this when I could wish—" He turned on his heel. "I must return to my work."

"Tobias!" Mistress Butler plucked at his sleeve. "May I have permission to sell the bowl that Emily has decorated so prettily? I can well make do with but one bowl."

"Or I could trade it to the wheelright," Nabby put in, "for the wheels."

Lonzo opened the door and stuck his head fearfully around the edge.

"Sir, a gentleman would have a word with you. No one was tending the shop, so he found his way to the workroom, where he awaits your pleasure."

Master Butler clapped a hand to his forehead. "The Reverend Morse come to inspect the church chalice I have had so long on my shelves. To think that I should forget!"

"The bowl?" Mistress Butler was not to be put off. "May I—"

"Yes, yes, yes, yes, whatever it is. Lonzo, stay and help the women dispose of this barrel as they will. It cannot, I presume, sit forever in the middle of the kitchen."

He disappeared down the passage to the workroom. Lonzo peered into the empty depths of the barrel.

"Yonder barrelhead is too large to fit the end of the barrel," he said scornfully. "The cooper has gulled you properly."

"You are clever to notice," said Nabby guilefully, "and you would be quite right if this were an ordinary barrel, but half of the front is to be cut away to the bulging midpoint, where the barrelhead will be fitted in to make a chair seat."

"A chair seat?" Lonzo circled the barrel and ran a hand over the wood. "So? It could be done." His face showed signs of interest for a moment but then turned sullen again. "Where do you want this barrel put? Master Butler will be roaring for me if I am gone longer than a moment."

"Lonzo," said Nabby, "was not your father a carpenter? And, given the right tools, could you not make this chair for us?" She offered her best argument. "And, if Master Butler agrees, would you not rejoice to be free of pewtering for a bit?"

"Our maiden voyage!" Nabby triumphantly eased Emily over the threshold in her rolling chair. "Where away first?"

"You must set our course since you are the skipper of this craft."

Emily's cheeks were scarlet with excitement as she waved at her mother and a few of the neighbors, gathered to see her set forth. Even Master Butler had left his work for a moment.

"Where is Lonzo?" Nabby asked. "Should he not be here to see his handiwork in use?"

Lonzo came, summoned by Master Butler. Surly-faced as always, he stared at his shoes while Emily smiled her thanks and even Master Butler said, "You have done well, boy." Mayhap surprised to hear himself praised, for once, Lonzo managed an awkward wave as Nabby pushed Emily, with her crutches tucked beside her, out onto Milk Street and up toward Marlborough.

"Stop!" cried Emily when the street was empty of spectators. "Please stop!"

Nabby bent over her. "You are not comfortable?

The chair bumps a bit, to be sure, but if I adjust the cushions—"

"No, 'tis not that!" Emily drew a little square of stiff paper from under the shawl that covered her legs. "I have christened our chair the 'Abigail Jonas,' and here is the touchmark." She smiled as Nabby admired a neat drawing of a ship, all sails set, with A.J., entwined with a length of ribbon, underneath. "I have never heard of a chair with a touchmark, but there is a first time for everything. Besides, you will need the design against the day when you make your own pewter."

That day would be a long time coming, but Nabby tried to match Emily's enthusiasm.

"The ship is exactly as I fancied it," she said slowly. "It is like your kindly heart to think of such a thing, though you give me too much credit. Lonzo built the chair, not I."

"But it was you who thought of it, and that is the important thing." Emily turned a radiant face on the new world around her. "And now I shall not talk but shall only look and listen. Is that the Old South Meeting House? And there is one of the new streetlamps you told me of. Oh, Nabby, I can hardly believe that I am out to see Boston at last."

Nabby could hardly believe it herself. It had taken nearly a month for all to be ready. Lonzo must build the chair and add handlebars by which Nabby would push it. Mistress Butler must find a buyer in the shop for the bowl with its band of wriggled work, for the wheelwright cared naught for pewter and must be paid only in cash. The wheels must be attached properly, with Will Truax and even Master Butler lending Lonzo a hand with that. Cushions must be fitted to the seat and back to ease the jolts. Even Emily, for all her wish to travel about the town, had had to be reassured.

"Everyone will stare," she had said doubtfully.

"Better be stared at for a day or so than stay housebound forever. Methinks everyone will envy you, with your own transportation, like a lady in a carriage."

"Like a fish in a barrel, rather." Emily drowned her misgivings in laughter. "I shall take paper and charcoal, and as everyone stares at me, I shall stare back at them and draw their pictures."

Today she had charcoal, a few broadsides, and a shingle on which to steady her paper, but Nabby doubted that she would be using them. She would be far too busy soaking up the sights of Boston—and what a day for it! The sky was blue and cloudless, and there was a Maytime scent of grass and new leaves, plus a whiff of fish from the harbor.

A jog left on Marlborough and up Summer to the Common, with its double row of trees forming the mall, and a few cows and sheep grazing placidly on the early spring grass—Nabby could have found something for Emily to see on every street. For today, though, she must pick and choose. Up one street and down the next, talking as she went, Nabby passed King's Chapel, the Green Dragon, Dock Square, and Faneuil Hall.

"Look up," said Nabby, "and see Faneuil's golden grasshopper glinting in the sun."

She doubled back a bit to pass the print shop, hoping to show Will Truax the Abigail Jonas in action for the first time. Glancing through the window, she saw a frenzied darting to and fro. Will, with his back to the street, was pulling the handle of the press, from which two journeymen were snatching sheets of paper as fast as they were printed.

"Another time," she told Emily. "After all, we have many a day for this. Shall we go now to see Mill Cove and the water mill?"

"Long Wharf, if you please," said Emily, bright-eyed. "I have dreamed of that since the first day you stepped into our house."

"Away then, to the wharf," said Nabby, delighted.

On Merchant's Row, a few faces peered from the business places as Emily's equipage passed. A large brown dog yapped but dared not venture close to her strange vehicle.

"And here," said Nabby, "is where King Street goes to sea and becomes Long Wharf."

As always, there was a tangle of people, all, it seemed, staring at Emily and the Abigail Jonas and buzz-buzzing to each other. Two British soldiers walked by with a burst of scornful laughter, quickly silenced by angry looks. Bostonians might laugh at other Bostonians, but British soldiers might not. Emily, surrounded by the hurly-burly of the wharf, seemed too entranced even to notice the glances turned in her direction.

Nabby drew a deep breath. The water was satiny blue, an echo of the sky, and sunlight danced on the ripples—Long Wharf and the harbor at their very best. From the far end of the wharf, she might even be able to show Emily how country boys in skiffs, with ropes and prods in hand, herded swimming cows from island to tiny island in search of fresh grazing.

"A ship!" cried Emily at sight of a square-rigger towering over her head. "I could almost reach out and touch it. Oh, and another and another and another! Show me, Nabby, where you once lived and stared all these ships in the face."

"There." Nabby hastily pushed Emily's chair out of the way of a horse-drawn dray and a man rolling a barrel of molasses toward one of the warehouses. "There, where the counting house is now." She gulped. "The garret window above was ours."

It all seemed very long ago now—the days of her mother's shop and her father's between-voyage visits, the creak of hawsers and the sound of water lapping the wharf at night. That time was past—and no use sighing over it.

"Nabby!" The Widow Parsons came flying out of her tobacco shop. "Would you pass an old neighbor by without stopping to give me even a glimpse of the wheeled chair? And this must be young Emily Butler, of whom I have heard so much. Step inside, do, even though only for a moment." She bustled ahead, helping to lift the chair over the low step. A red-and-green parrot on a perch greeted them with a loud squawk and a gabble of talk. "A seaman just back from the West Indies left the bird here while he takes his ease in the grog shop. He—the parrot, that is—speaks only the outlandish language of his own country, so he is not the best of company."

She hastened to wait on a sailor who came in demanding a twist of tobacco.

"Pray push me closer, Nabby." The parrot stared unblinkingly as Emily took out her drawing materials. "A quick sketch of you, my pretty, for my last drawing of a parrot was as like as a barrel is to a candlestick."

"Have you heard aught of the *Boston Traveller?*" Nabby asked as the seaman turned to go.

"Nay, maid. His Majesty's ship the *Lively* was to sail for Boston a day behind ours, but the *Traveller* was still waiting, as we all must do, for her cargo."

Nabby gave a nod of satisfaction. Silas Bridges would have had time, then, to search out more much-needed tin for Master Butler.

"The *Lively* is here?"

"So I hear." His look evaded hers. "The talk is— But that is men's business, not young maids'."

Nabby glared after him. "Men's business, indeed! Have we not, women and all, grown accustomed to bad news from England? And dealt with it too—so far. Emily, if you have finished with that parrot, let us go forth into the sunshine."

"Pray come and visit me again," the Widow Parsons urged. "Sometimes I see only seamen and tobacco for days on end."

"And now and then a parrot," Emily murmured as Nabby maneuvered the chair outside.

The wharf was now more crowded than ever. Somewhere the town crier was shouting, too far away for Nabby to make out the words. Near the end of King Street, Will Truax, surrounded by people, was

passing out handbills left and right. Followed by a chorus of voices, he made his way onto the wharf.

"The chair!" Nabby hailed him as eager hands snatched at the broadsides. "Will, note the chair, how well it goes! And what things we have seen today!"

He gave the girls only a passing glance. "Best look while you may," he said gloomily, "for after June 1 no ship may enter Boston Harbor, and those already here must leave by June 14. The king and the milords in the Parliament have ordered the port closed." He thrust a broadside into Nabby's hands and raised his voice to the crowd. "Ill news! Ill news! Come read! Come read!"

"The port closed?" Nabby echoed his words. "But how— What—"

"No ships?" The Widow Parsons rushed into the street to see what befell. "Why, as well condemn Boston to death."

Angry voices rose around them.

"Never will this be endured!"

"Sam Adams and Dr. Warren will have something to say, and that right soon."

Tears blurred Emily's eyes.

"There, there!" Nabby patted her hand. "There will be a way to set all right." She did not quite believe her own cheery words, but she was determined not to let Emily's bright day be ruined. She folded the broadside and tucked it into her pocket. "We will take this at once to your father, who may by now have further news, and tomorrow we will visit the smaller wharves, lest indeed—" Her voice trailed away at the thought that Will might be right and that there would soon be no ships to see in Boston.

Master Butler had already heard the news, brought, as the seaman had hinted, by the *Lively*.

"The port is to be closed to mercantile shipping, both coming and going, until the tea we threw into the sea is paid for," he said in a voice of cold fury, "a day that will never come, methinks. Salem is to replace Boston as the capital of the colony, and the customs house will be moved to Plymouth. Governor Hutchinson will go to London to report to the king, and General Gage will take over as governor of Massachusetts in his absence, with added British regiments to help him close the port and keep order. And so they will try to starve us into submission."

There was more news the next day and the next, and Nabby and Emily fared forth daily to hear it, although none of it was good. Indignation meetings, committees, resolutions—Boston, even for those who remained loyal to the king, was like a nest of angry hornets. Paul Revere rode express again to New York and Philadelphia, taking with him broadsides, designed by himself, of the Boston Port Bill, with a skull and crossbones and other mournful trimmings.

"We are not to starve, after all—quite," Master Butler reported after one of the meetings that kept him often from home just as before the tea party. "Food and necessary fuel may be brought coastwise, though how they are to be paid for, I do not know. With no commercial shipping, there will be no work for the men on the wharves, nor will the merchants have much to sell, even if anyone has the money to buy. I look to see thousands without employment—and those thousands will be bent on trouble, mark my words. I do not doubt that Sam Adams is devising means to turn their rebellious mood to the aid of our beleaguered town."

"And what of your pewtering?" Nabby asked.

"I can count on no more tin from Silas Bridges unless the *Boston Traveller* makes port before June 1, which I think unlikely. We must make do with old pewter melted down—the same old story." His voice slowed. "It irks me to put my touchmark on work that is not the very best, all for want of proper metal."

At least he might have a larger supply of old pewter to work with in the fall when Jeremiah Curtin returned from his peddling. Nabby must mention that to Master Butler when he was not so caught up in other matters.

"And if there are no customers?" Nabby persisted.

"I believe there will be some, though not as many as we could wish, and that, too, is hardly an unusual state of affairs. There are men of means on the patriots' side, but their minds will be on other things than pewter. Mayhap the British officers who will head all these regiments with which we are to be afflicted may be a source of custom." His look turned grim. "Lead may be in especially short supply ere long, although I shall not give up hope that it may turn out otherwise."

Nabby and Emily exchanged questioning glances, but Master Butler hurried back to his workroom, where Lonzo would have the forge ready for whatever alloy Master Butler could manage with what he had at hand. Nabby looked wistfully after him. Now that

Emily could go traveling, she chose to do so daily. Nabby, who had always yearned to be out and away, now wished perversely that she were oftener at home, to be summoned sometimes into the workroom to hear Master Butler discoursing about pewter or, on lucky days, to help him in some small way. Never would she become a pewterer at this rate. She had hopefully pictured both herself and Emily established in the workroom, Emily decorating a piece of pewter held firmly in the vise and Nabby herself ladling metal into a mold.

It was not a time for this kind of dreaming nowadays, however, for the streets of Boston surged with color and excitement that must not be missed. General Gage arrived not long after the *Lively* and reviewed a correct but unenthusiastic militia on Long Wharf in a chilly rain. He was accompanied by four regiments of troops, some of whom set up their tents on the Common.

With only a short time to clear the harbor of shipping, the wharves, both big and small, were in a frantic bustle of activity. Merchants desperately brought last-minute cargoes into Boston. Foodstuffs and wood arrived by barge. Shipowners hurried to unload their craft and rush them to safety in Marblehead and Salem. Emily made a sketch of a grizzled seaman, who tossed her a penny for it.

"If only I had proper paper, I might make sketches to put in the shop alongside my father's pewter and mayhap sell a few," said Emily.

"So you might," Nabby agreed. "I will consult Will Truax, who may know where heavy white paper may be had." She sighed. "There again we have the problem of paying for it."

In the meantime, Emily sketched everything she saw—ships, soldiers, bewildered seamen—on the backs of the plentiful broadsides that were distributed throughout the town.

"They can be copied later onto something better," she said hopefully.

Nabby had no interest in sketches as she watched the wharves emptying day by day of the ships that had given Boston its life and flavor for as long as she could remember. On the day the Port Bill went into effect, hardly a vessel was to be seen in the harbor except the warships that would keep the town bottled up and the transports that brought in ever more Royal troops.

"The bells!" cried Nabby as she wheeled Emily past vacant wharves. "Hear the bells!" Every church bell in Boston was tolling in sorrow. Nabby's eyes filled with tears despite her determination to keep up a brave front. "Oh, Emily, 'tis a sad day for Boston!"

She shed no more futile tears as the days passed and Boston remained sunk in gloom. She and Emily wandered from wharf to wharf among angry men who had little to do except to watch the soldiers who came pouring into town, filling the air with the sound of drums and the clump-clump of their boots.

Bostonians, with a long memory for past events, had long taken pleasure in plaguing British soldiers, who did not hesitate to fight back, but now there was an uneasy peace, not even interrupted by the Sons of Liberty, always spoiling for a fight.

"We are close to being outnumbered, anyway,"

Nabby remarked one day when she and Emily met Will Truax in front of the Liberty Tree, which was hung with broadsides. "Besides, the soldiers seem better behaved than before."

"On General Gage's orders, so we hear," said Will. "Emily, my master says he may be able to lay hands on some better paper for your drawings, but not soon."

"Not soon will be soon enough, I fear," said Nabby. "Do you think he might allow her to pay for the paper when she has sold a few of the drawings?"

"I will ask. How fares it with Master Butler?"

"Not well," said Nabby, "though not so badly as for many others."

Master Butler, with his dwindling funds, was able to buy a piece of old pewter here and another there, sold, as often as not, to put food in hungry mouths.

"I would pay twice too much if my means would allow," he mourned.

At least food was available as word spread of Boston's sorry plight. Rice came from the Carolinas, sheep from Connecticut, flour from Quebec, money from everywhere, and jobs in nearby towns for a few of the unemployed. The selectmen tried to supply work for some of the rest so that they might pay for their food by paving streets, cleaning docks, and repairing wharves. Boston merchants were offered the use of wharves in Salem and Marblehead, from whence they brought their goods by cart over the Neck into town.

"A drop in the bucket," Master Butler said, "compared to Boston's golden days of shipping."

He was cheered in midsummer when a country-man came bumbling into the kitchen at dusk one evening with some highly scented fish in a basket.

"From Silas Bridges in Salem," he whispered hoarsely.

"Fish?" said Nabby, but Master Butler exclaimed, "In Boston nowadays we welcome food of any sort."

Glancing at Lonzo, who was finishing his meal, he drew the countryman outside into the summer darkness. There was the faint clink of coins, and the next morning Master Butler said, "Nabby, may I borrow your porringer to show today to a gentleman who may wish to order one with a flowered handle like yours?" He winked behind Lonzo's back. "I have come upon a few scraps of tin to improve the miserable alloy I have had to work with of late."

Nabby hastened to fetch the porringer before she and Emily started for Long Wharf to see the Widow Parsons. A rainstorm caught them midway there, and Nabby pushed the chair back at top speed. She found Mistress Butler away and Master Butler in the sales shop, talking to a young man whom Nabby had never seen before.

"I bid you good day," Master Butler was saying, "and mayhap I may be able to find help of the kind you need. Nabby, when you have settled Emily in her place, I would have a word with you."

A word about what? Nabby could not help feeling uneasy as she shepherded Emily into the kitchen.

"Lonzo!" Master Butler lifted his voice toward the workroom. "Make ready the forge, collect our stray bits of old pewter, and throw them into the pot. Today we will make up for lost time and fill a few orders."

Nabby helped Emily to the settle in the kitchen and brought her a dry petticoat and smock.

"Even a rainstorm is a joy," said Emily, "for one who has never been caught in one before."

Nabby went with lagging steps to the shop, from which Mistress Butler was still absent.

"Your customer gave you the order for the porringer, then?" she asked, thinking to distract Master Butler's mind from that "word" he was planning to have with her.

"An exact copy of yours, only larger, and I am to make a teapot as well. Now, as to—"

"Sir," Nabby interrupted, "may I fetch my porringer from the workroom? I—I feel that ill luck may befall me without it."

She fled down the hall to the workroom.

"Oh, Lonzo, no!"

Ill luck, indeed! Lonzo was just dropping Nabby's porringer into the melting pot.

"My porringer!" With a scream of outrage, Nabby flung herself at Lonzo and pushed him aside with a jab of her elbow. Snatching the ladle that Master Butler used to fill the molds, she scooped up the porringer just as it was sinking into the hot metal in the pot. Bits of molten pewter dripped from the ladle as Nabby eased the porringer onto the worktable. "See what you have done! The touchmark partly blotted out and half the handle melted away!" She rounded on Lonzo with a resounding slap and burst into angry tears. "The only thing I ever had that—"

"What is this?" Master Butler strode through the doorway. "A pair of angry wildcats? Have I not warned you time and again that I will brook no more quarreling?"

He was greeted by a babble of words. "He was melting down my porringer!" Nabby wailed.

"You said to drop the old pewter into the pot, and the porringer was lying there with the rest." Lonzo's face was as innocent as a new-laid egg.

"Lying where?" Nabby demanded. "You *knew* it was my porringer, too fine to be melted down as scrap."

"How should I know it was yours?" Lonzo fingered his cheek, reddened from Nabby's slap. "I have heard a world of talk about this porringer, but I never set eyes on it until—"

"Until when? Until you saw Master Butler showing the design to his customer today."

"Leave off this railing, both of you!" said Master Butler. "Lonzo, you showed a spiteful spirit in trying to destroy Nabby's porringer—if you knew it was hers, as I suspect you did. If you did not, but took it for scrap, you showed deplorable ignorance of good pewter, despite my efforts to teach you." He glanced at Nabby's stormy face. "As for you, slapping and screaming are far from attractive in a young maid, and, worse, seldom gain your purpose." He paused. "I fear I was remiss myself in leaving another's property where it might come to harm, so we are all at fault in greater or lesser degree. Now let me look at the porringer. Mayhap we can repair it." He turned it over and over. "No small task, I fear, the handle especially. As for the touchmark— Ah, well, we shall see, but now I must start molding the parts for the teapot, a wearisome task." Nevertheless, he had an air of pleasant anticipation. "I have not made one for many a day, lacking both proper metal and an order."

Nabby picked up the damaged porringer. "I will keep it by me," she said in a muffled voice, "until you have time to work on it."

"Do so," Master Butler said absently. "Now, Lonzo, at last we will have an opportunity to use the new teapot molds."

For once, Nabby was not interested in new molds.

Moreover, Master Butler had not invited her to stay and watch, nor did she think she could endure even being in the same room with Lonzo.

"Why?" she asked Emily as they sat talking in the kitchen. "Why would he do such a thing? Naturally he was angry that I substituted parsley for his tea back in December, but did I not do him a good turn later by persuading your father to let him make your chair for you? While he was working at that, he seemed almost cheerful, and he should be at least a little grateful for the chance." She looked mournfully at her porringer. "A sorry sight."

Emily studied the porringer. "Do you think I could restore the touchmark with wriggled work? It would not be as deeply impressed as it was, but at least it would be better than it is now."

"If Master Butler cannot repair the handle, it will not matter whether there is a touchmark or not. Whoever made the porringer would not wish his touch to remain on damaged work."

Emily's face puckered. "I feel very like your porringer sometimes," she whispered, "as though my father wishes he could withhold his mark from something so flawed and broken."

"Oh, Emily! That is not the way of it. We all have our flaws, every one, some in body, some otherwise. Did I not make a spectacle of myself just now by screaming like a fishwife at Lonzo?"

"Who deserved it." Emily rose stoutly to her defense.

"And more. But your father said he was at fault,

too, for leaving my porringer where it might come to harm."

"He did?" said Emily in amazement.

"He did. And I cannot but think that he is proud of your skill with the wriggled work. It is just that—"

"That I am a daughter, not a son."

"And sons are ever more cherished." Nabby managed a wry smile. "I do not wish to *be* a boy but only to be allowed to—"

"To become a pewterer," said Emily.

"When I do, you shall decorate my teapots with wriggled work." Nabby launched into her favorite subject. "When you are not doing that, you shall hold the mold while I pour in the molten metal or you may sit at the lathe to burnish the pewter while I turn the wheel."

"Oh, Nabby, could I? Could I truly do all that?"

"Why not?" Nabby pressed her nose to the windowpane, down which rain continued to stream. "Blessings on the storm, at least, for bringing me home in time to save my porringer from being melted entirely." She smiled. "The British soldiers encamped in tents on the Common are not blessing the rain, I warrant." Every day they drilled and marched except in such weather as this, when they were doubtless miserably bemired in the mud. "I could almost feel sorry for them, save that they were sent to Boston either to rule or ruin."

"And like to succeed, too." Master Butler sank wearily onto the bench in the kitchen. "Nabby, I want to talk to you." Nabby's heart sank. Here was the "word" that she had hoped was forgotten. "And to Emily."

"To me?" Emily gave Nabby a puzzled look.

"Whatever we did," Nabby blurted, "we meant no harm."

"Nay, girl, nothing like that. The patriot cause needs observers who can roam at will through the streets of Boston, listen in the right places, and, if need arises, carry messages back and forth."

"Back and forth where?" Nabby demanded suspiciously.

"How do I know? Our thought was that the two of you are becoming an accustomed sight in Boston, and no one would—"

"Suspect our foul purposes?" Nabby said with relish. "For myself, I would be glad enough to help, but I would not wish to lead Emily into danger."

"Would I ask you to do it if it would endanger either of you? It is simply a matter of walking past the Common and other places, as half the populace does every day, and telling me what you see and hear. Any messages that you might be asked to carry would be so well hidden that no one would know of them."

"Not in that teapot again, I hope," said Nabby. "Pray recall that I found whatever it was, and anyone else could have, too."

"Luckily no one did, and now it is safely stowed with Master Edes, who will keep it hidden forever if need be." He lowered his voice. "It was a partial list of those who threw the tea overboard and the tasks they were to perform—not a document that should fall into British hands."

"If I were sending a message in a teapot," Nabby went on, "I would make it out like a bill for pewter work, with each figure having a special meaning. Emily and I could work out a cipher for you."

"I daresay," said Master Butler.

Nabby began at once to organize the project further. "Since Emily stops and sketches so often, we will have a good excuse for being almost anywhere."

"I can see," said Master Butler, "that you will be of great help to us."

Nabby gave him a long look, unsure whether his words were to be taken at face value. "Shall we start tomorrow?" Hardly drawing breath, she added, "If so, I can leave my porringer with you then, so you may see whether it can be mended."

He looked at her with a glint of amusement. "You have early grasped one of the secrets of success: press every advantage. You may leave the porringer since one favor deserves another."

"You will not let it out of your sight?"

"I promise."

"And I promise we will return with news of some sort."

The most important news that they returned with was news that Master Butler and the whole town of Boston knew as soon as Nabby and Emily did.

"The last straw in a haystack of oppression," said Will Truax when he met the girls near the Common. He gave Nabby a sheepish look when she burst out laughing at his flowery talk. " 'Twas not I who coined the phrase but my master, who has a way with words."

"Very well, what *is* this last straw?" Nabby asked.

"The Quartering Act, latest edict from London. British soldiers may now be quartered in any man's house if enough barracks cannot be provided for them elsewhere in the town."

"They will know everything we do," said Nabby, horrified.

Will grinned at her. "On the other hand, we will know everything *they* do. I hear the patriots are recruiting observers on every hand."

Nabby looked around her. "Where?" she demanded. "Oh, I see one under my nose now, a red-haired one of long experience."

Will sobered. "Best take care today," he said. "A rock narrowly missed one of the soldiers just now, and it will not be the last one."

"Oh, but we are observers, and so we must observe," Nabby argued.

"Somewhere else in the town might do as well." Emily shrank back into the curved shelter of the barrel chair.

Still Nabby lingered, watching soldiers drilling in scarlet lines across the Common.

"I hear," a passing artisan said to his companion, "that they plan to build more barracks against the winter, but where will they find carpenters to work? No patriot would lift a hammer to help. As for me, I would favor tearing the barracks down as fast as they are built."

"And be hung for it. Still, they can force no man to work for them—or can they?"

"A bit of news already for my father," Emily said with satisfaction.

"Quick! Get out your drawing things," Nabby whispered. "Yonder comes a couple who might be subjects for a sketch."

A lady in a dashingly tilted bonnet and a flounced silk dress was approaching on the arm of a British officer. Nabby stepped into their path.

"May I ask a great favor, milady? My friend here has a talent for drawing and fain would sketch you in your lovely gown—and your escort, too. It would take but a few moments, and she does not often have a chance to draw so handsome a couple."

Nabby almost choked on these honeyed words, but they did the trick. The lady's eyebrows arched.

"What think you, Francis? It might be amusing." She caught sight of Emily's crutches. "Why, the girl is— Of course! Where shall we stand?"

"There, beside this bush," Nabby directed. "Take note, Emily, of the plumes on the bonnet and—"

Emily, red-faced either from excitement or suppressed laughter, sketched busily.

"I regret that the sketch paper is only the back of a handbill," said Nabby, "but good paper is hard to come by."

"No matter." The lady, carefully smiling, stood chatting with her escort, apparently about the parties at which those loyal to the crown were entertaining the British officers. Nabby, hovering as though admiring the lady's attire, caught only scattered words.

"The dance . . . September 1?" the officer murmured. "The talk is . . . General Gage . . . about that time . . . Charlestown . . . when he will . . ."
He raised his voice. "But why bother your pretty head

about such things? Let us be off. 'Tis like your soft heart to humor a poor cripple, but—"

Two red spots appeared on Emily's cheeks as she bent over her drawing, with the charcoal clenched between her fingers. Nabby hastened to take the sketch and show it to the lady.

"Unfinished work," she said, "but is it not very like? And we thank you for sparing us the time."

"Very pretty," the lady said in a perfunctory tone. "Francis, give the girl a coin. I will keep the sketch to show at my next tea party."

She swished away, and Nabby laid a soothing hand on Emily's arm.

"Pay no heed. Some of the gentry, I hear, tend to talk as though everybody else is invisible. I think she meant to be kind."

"A sorry sort of kindness," Will growled.

"And you have a bit of money now," Nabby persisted. "You can buy paper with it if you will. Come, wipe your tears. We gathered another item of information, which will please your father."

"What information?"

"Why, that there is something going on at Charlestown that General Gage is concerned with or will be soon."

"I will tell my master, too," said Will.

"And pray that he does not send you on the Charlestown ferry to find out what betides," said Nabby.

"Easier said than done," Will said cheerfully. "The ferry was closed for a time, a kind deed for which I cannot but thank the British, and now it is watched too closely for comfort—if there is ever any comfort to be found on the water." He frowned. "Did you note what was on the back of that sketch? Though broadsides are everywhere, it would be best for your purposes not to advertise yourselves as sympathetic to rebellion."

"True for you!" said Nabby. "I think there was only a smudge of ink from the press on that particular piece of paper, but I will take heed for the future. As you say, it is safer for us to appear to be only a girl with an artistic gift and the servant who pushes her about."

"A servant!" Emily cried. "A dear friend, rather!"

The girls diligently roamed the streets of Boston, listening every day for scraps of talk. Two British soldiers fought with an artisan in the grog shop next to the Widow Parsons'. Stores for General Gage's men mysteriously disappeared. Provincial militia, purged of those loyal to the crown, were drilling on village greens all around the Massachusetts countryside. Samuel and John Adams were soon to leave for Philadelphia to represent Massachusetts at the First Continental Congress, called to discuss Britain's oppressive measures. Town-owned gunpowder was being spirited away from powderhouses across the Charles to safekeeping elsewhere, and the villagers were looking yearningly at that belonging to the king.

"Since that first lucky day, we have learned little that everybody else does not know," Nabby said fretfully.

Rather to her own surprise, she was growing weary of spending most of her waking hours looking at things she had been seeing all her life. Carriages imported from England by the gentry still swept down the streets to such shops as had merchandise to sell. To Emily's delight, the little boys busily guided their swimming cows to island grazing. Men milled around Long Wharf as before, though with no need now to duck around carts and drays. Women went to market with their baskets on their arms, bargaining for fish and meal.

Emily, enchanted by it all, never tired of her daily expeditions in the Abigail Jonas. She grew rosy under the summer sun and bright-eyed from fresh air and the excitement of exploring the wide world. She made sketches as she went, sometimes on the heavier paper that Will's master had found for her and sometimes, more often, on tattered handbills. Now and then a British soldier gave her a coin for a sketch to be sent home to England, money that went for more paper. As for the wriggled work, she seemed to have forgotten that entirely.

Even the reports of what the girls had seen and heard each day must be given not in the workroom but in the kitchen after Lonzo had left. He always ate rapidly and in silence and then vanished into the darkness. Master Butler would stare after him and shrug.

"His time after he does his day's work is his own, true, but still I am responsible for him. I fear he is up to no good."

Nabby cared naught for what Lonzo was doing. If he was indeed making mischief, he would be caught at it sooner or later.

"And good enough for him," she murmured to Emily, "for ruining my porringer!"

The porringer had not yet been repaired, despite Master Butler's promises.

"I do not have metal of a quality to match the original," he said, "so I must ask your patience a little longer."

He had had good pewter for the teapot he had started the day Nabby's porringer was damaged, but had he saved even a scrap of it for Nabby? Of course not. He seemed to read her angry thoughts.

"I had taken the order for the teapot before disaster befell your porringer," he said. "In business matters, it must be first come, first served. You stand next in line for the superior alloy that is all I would use on a top-quality porringer."

Nabby frowned. She was happy to know she had such a superior porringer, but who knew how long it would be before the *Boston Traveller* brought more tin to sweeten the alloy?

"Nabby!" Master Butler called when the girls came wearily home one day. "Pray bring Emily to the workroom."

He appeared to be in high good humor as usually he was not.

"Emily, a lady on Summer Street saw the bowl with the wriggled work and has ordered one like it, except that she would like to see a different design. She is, I believe, partial to garlands of flowers."

"An order!" Nabby burst out. "Did I not say so?"

"You did." Master Butler turned again to Emily. "When you have drawn the design and I have had it approved, I will make a place for you to work here, with the vise close at hand to hold the bowl firmly."

"And with Nabby to help me?" asked Emily.

"I will give you what little help you will need my-self—or Lonzo will. I have other plans for Nabby."

Nabby swallowed her disappointment and guided Emily and the wheeled chair into the kitchen. The sound of a deep voice from the workroom drew her back to peer through the crack in the half-open door.

"Master Butler? My name is Jeremiah Curtin, the peddler, and I have both news and goods for you." He sat himself down at the workbench without so much as a by-your-leave. "The news, in case you have not heard, is that a party of British soldiers rowed up the Mystic River this morning, marched to the powder-house in Charlestown, and brought the king's powder back to Castle William before the townspeople could make off with it themselves. Rebel militia are swarm-ing from every direction, too late by far and twice as angry to make up for it."

September 1! Charlestown! Nabby could have cried if she had been the weeping kind. To think that she and Emily and Will had all had a hint of this ex-pedition from the British officer only a short time ago and never a whisper since!

"Now, as to the pewter," Jeremiah Curtin went on, "I have brought you all I could find, to be melted down as the girl agreed, and I will be glad to take a newly made supply for sale when I go peddling in the spring if we can come to terms."

"Pewter? 'The girl agreed'?" Master Butler's voice was bewildered for a moment, but then it rose to a familiar roar. "Nabby! Nabby! What meddlesome tricks have you been up to now?"

10

"*Too much lead by far.*" Master Butler drew one of Jeremiah Curtin's spoons across a scrap of paper. "The darker the mark, the more lead and the poorer the pewter."

"If it does not suit, I can dispose of it elsewhere," Jeremiah Curtin said airily. "For certain uses nowadays, the more lead the better."

Master Butler gave him a sharp look. "Hardly a use suitable for a pewterer."

"But for a patriot?" Jeremiah Curtin remained unruffled.

Nabby was all ears. Having made her explanation about what she had told Jeremiah Curtin in the spring, she had retreated to the far corner of the workroom to think over the words she had so carefully chosen to soothe Master Butler's ruffled temper.

"It seemed a great opportunity," she had said meekly. "You are always in need of more pewter and of more business, too, and Master Curtin's visits to faraway settlements would help with both. I had intended to speak of it to you, but I was waiting for a time when—"

When Master Butler was in a good mood, which was seldom enough. He had waved her to silence and had turned to inspect the battered pewter that the peddler had brought. At the end of the dickering, Master Butler scraped up enough money to buy every piece.

"I will use most of it for something you can sell on your return trip in the spring," he told Jeremiah Curtin, "for trade is poor here in Boston and likely to be poorer. What items will go best among your customers?"

"Plates, spoons, and bowls for the householders, and tankards for the inns and taverns. The poorest quality of metal you may prefer to save for the use I spoke of." He nodded in Nabby's direction as he rose to go. "You have a shrewd dealer there," a remark that earned Nabby a hard look from Lonzo and only a curt nod from Master Butler. "Did I tell you that, besides the ammunition at Charlestown, Gage's men also seized two brass cannon in Cambridge before the citizens could hide them away?"

"A triumph for Gage," said Master Butler, "but I warrant he will be hard put to it to mount such an expedition in secret again. Our Boston men, with little work, thanks to the British, will spend even more time watching and listening now."

There was a deal to watch, too. General Gage ordered four large field pieces brought from the Common to guard the Neck, the only land approach to Boston. The frigate *Lively* moved into the ferryway to Charlestown, and three men-of-war hovered nearby. The object, according to Will, was to keep Boston bottled up and prevent the rebels in the country outside from coming to the town's rescue either by water or over the Neck.

"Need I continue all this looking and listening?" Nabby asked Master Butler the evening after Jeremiah Curtin's visit. "There are a hundred others doing the same and with better luck."

Besides, she had rather be with Emily, busy with her wriggled work.

"Very well," said Master Butler, "you may run an errand of another sort tomorrow, and Emily shall go with you. Do you recall the old abandoned wharf from which there is so close a view of the little harbor islands?"

"Where the cows swim," said Emily, now almost as familiar as Nabby with Boston and its harbor.

"Exactly." Master Butler took a pewter dram bottle down from the shelf. "Pray go forth as early as may be tomorrow and hand this bottle to Will Truax."

Nabby stared at him. "A bottle? To Will Truax?"

"Who will know what to do with it. Now to bed, both of you, so you may arise betimes. Tomorrow you will take care to appear as though you are only out for your daily stroll. No, do not take the bottle abovestairs with you. It will be ready for you in the morning."

Nabby went to bed with her head in a whirl. Why could Will not come for the bottle himself? And why a dram bottle, of all things? And what would Will do with it, once he had it? Some kind of message was involved, she supposed, but a dram bottle was an unlikely place for a note. Master Butler should have let her and Emily work out a cipher as she had suggested.

She tossed all night long until the morning sun glinted on her porringer and Mistress Butler came to help carry Emily downstairs.

"A fine day for faring forth," Master Butler said genially with an eye on Lonzo, who was finishing his bowl of mush.

"Indeed, yes." Nabby picked up the hint. "We shall wander here and there like a—a pair of butter-flies." When Lonzo had gone to mend the forge fire, Nabby said, "Sir, where—"

"You will find the bottle tucked behind one of the cushions of Emily's equipage. Pray bring back, with equal secrecy, what Will Truax gives you."

He strode into his workroom, and Nabby hastened to help Emily into the Abigail Jonas and through the door.

"Should we not make sure that all is well with the bottle?" Nabby asked when they were well out of sight of the house. "We would not wish to deliver it in poor condition."

Emily giggled. "Or without finding what is in it. In the shadow of yonder tree would be a safe place— and the street is empty just now."

The bottle, retrieved from behind the cushion at Emily's back, looked perfectly ordinary, a round, shallow flask to hold a dram of spirits, with a threaded metal stopper in the neck and no touchmark. A crude *CH 9 8* was scratched on the bottom. Nabby hesitated.

"Mayhap we should not—"

" 'Should' or not, pray unstop it," said Emily. "I cannot endure not knowing what is inside."

The stopper refused to budge until Nabby turned it with her teeth, leaving a row of marks on the soft pewter and a taste of metal in her mouth. She peered inside.

"A dram of spirits, nothing else," she said in disappointment. "Indeed, I expected a note." She dipped a finger into the liquid and touched it to her lips. "Why, 'tis only water, and what is the sense of that? Oh!"

She screwed the stopper hastily back in place as a frowning man in a flat hat and a black coat approached.

"Strong drink ill befits young maids," he said piously, "and on a public street, too."

"Oh, sir, 'tis naught but a cooling draft of water." Nabby held out the bottle to him. "See for yourself. We are out for an airing and will be long from home."

He sniffed at the bottle and, with an air of doubt, walked on. Nabby hastily tucked the bottle behind Emily's cushion again.

"What a fright!" she said, conscience-stricken. "Oh, Emily, your father trusted us, and my curiosity led me astray again."

"And mine helped," Emily said, "but where's the harm? We found no secrets in the bottle, and so none were given away. Mayhap we will have better luck with whatever Will Truax gives us in exchange."

"Emily, you are a worse villain than I," said Nabby.

Will, empty-handed, came out from the shadow of a shed beside the abandoned wharf.

"You have something for me?" he asked miserably. "I could wish that you did not, for I must take it in yonder aged skiff"—he shuddered—"to meet a boy in a green-painted boat towing a brown-and-white cow to forage on the smallest of the islands."

Nabby's spirits lifted. She could row a boat, and she never got seasick.

"I would be glad to go in your place," she said eagerly, but Will shook his head.

"I have my orders. Give me the dram bottle."

Tight-lipped, he climbed into the skiff. Nabby pushed it out from shore, sorely tempted at the last moment to leap into the boat herself. He seemed to sense her intention.

"Remember Emily. She is your duty. This is mine."

She was ashamed to have forgotten, though even without Emily to look after, she doubted that Will would have let her go with him. A boy, yes, but never a girl. She watched as Will set an erratic course toward the littlest island.

"A landsman born and bred," she said. "He would have saved himself a few moments asea if he had not started until he sighted the green boat and the cow." She squinted across the sparkling water. "I do believe— Emily, is that a green boat?"

Emily nodded. "And a swimming cow, though I cannot make out its color."

"Half the cows in Massachusetts are brown and white," said Nabby, "and the other half are white and brown." She clutched Emily's arm. "Out with the charcoal and paper and start sketching cows! I see a British soldier approaching."

He was not one of the hard-faced, grizzled veterans but young and awkward.

"Yonder boat," he said abruptly. "Who is in it, and where is it bound?"

"What boat?" Nabby asked. "We have just arrived to draw pictures of this pretty scene."

"The skiff that just put out from here. A red-haired boy is at the oars."

Nabby shrugged. "Mayhap he is going fishing, for food is scarce for ordinary folk nowadays. Sometimes, too, friends from the countryside bring a few eggs or a bit of meat for their friends when they swim the cows to the islands. Why, only last week my mistress had a basket of—"

Of dried codfish bought at the market, but talk might distract the soldier's mind. Out of the corner of her eye Nabby saw the green boat landing on the pebbly shingle and the brown-and-white cow floundering ashore in search of fresh pasture. She hoped that Will, pulling up alongside the green boat, would note the scarlet of the soldier's uniform and take heed. The figures of Will and the lad who climbed out of the other boat were so much reduced by distance that it was only by squinting that Nabby could see Will offering the other boy the dram bottle. He tilted it to his lips. Nabby heaved a sigh of relief. Seasick though he doubtless was, Will had managed to set the scene for the British soldier, who was shading his eyes with his hand as he looked out over the water.

"A dram of something ne'er goes amiss between friends," said Nabby, "for friends they must be. Emily,

I see a boat with two cows and a horse following astern. Pray sketch that; otherwise, your father will never believe such a tale."

Emily bent to her work, and Nabby looked calmly out to the island. Now the lad from the green boat was handing a market basket to Will.

"Lucky boy!" Nabby exclaimed. "Someone will have a good supper tonight."

The British soldier, with a final look, walked away.

"Now let us hope that he does not come back and prevent Will from giving us whatever it is that we must return to your father," said Nabby.

She watched Will zigzagging leisurely past one island after another like a boy with nothing on his mind except exploring. Eventually he pulled the boat in around a curve in the shore, well south of where he had started.

"A clever maneuver," she said, "to throw off any watcher who might think he had any other intent than to enjoy a sunny morning on the water. Put away your drawing things, and we will go home and consult your father."

As they were walking down Cow Lane, they sighted Will, so pale that his freckles stood out like dabs of paint. His red hair was now covered with a countryman's wide-brimmed hat, and he was carrying the market basket on his arm.

"Apples from the countryside! Potatoes! Fresh-ground meal!" he called, with no sign of recognizing the girls. "Pray look!"

He set the basket on Emily's lap. Watching carefully for observers, he drew from under the apples and potatoes a cloth-wrapped rectangular package, which he whisked behind Emily's back cushion. He was just in time, too, for a woman came hurrying out of her house, saying, "Here, boy! I am in need of meal and mayhap a few potatoes if they are not too dear."

Without a word, Will took the basket and hurried over to his prospective customer. Nabby pushed the wheeled chair toward home as Emily moved restlessly against the cushions.

"Whatever it is, it is as hard as a rock," she said. "Metal, I think, two or three inches wide and a foot or so long, with"—she eased herself to the far side of the chair—"handles at this end."

"Can it be," said Nabby, "that all that skulduggery was for naught save to deliver a new mold to your father?"

But a mold for what? She was not to find out, for the street was never empty, and Will, swinging his empty market basket, followed them at a distance until he saw they were safely home. There Master Butler took possession of the package with only a "Many thanks" and took it into the workroom.

Emily, busy the next day with still another order for wriggled work, reported no sign of anything the size and shape of the mysterious package. Nabby set forth unwillingly for her daily stroll, this time to Boston Neck, where a crowd of idle workers were jeering at the added fortifications that were going up inch by inch.

"Beaver dams!" an artisan said gleefully. "One kick and over they'll go!"

"Workers are being sent for from Nova Scotia," another said, "else the job would never be done."

As Nabby darted around the edges of the crowd to find a good vantage point, she almost collided with Lonzo, who was staring as though bewitched at a mason or two laying brick and a few hangdog carpenters.

"Did not Master Butler send you out to deliver three plates in the North End?" Nabby demanded.

"I have already delivered them, if you must know!" Lonzo said defiantly. "I ran all the way so I could come and see what is being built here." He gave her a little push. "Hurry back to Master Butler now and give him another black mark to put against my name."

"I care naught what you do as long as the pewter is delivered." Besides, she had raced through the streets many a time herself to save a few moments for pleasure on the way home. "Come, I will walk back with you to Master Butler's. Mayhap I can watch him working on the clock face he is making."

"Pewter, pewter, pewter!" Lonzo burst out. "I am sick of the very word."

"That I do not doubt." Nabby matched him stride for stride. "You had been better apprenticed to a carpenter, for I see that building holds your interest where pewter does not."

"Aye. I would have worked with my father, but when he died, there was no carpenter in need of an apprentice." He scowled. "It was my bad luck that I should be apprenticed to Master Butler, where I get only hard words, while you—"

"You have no love for pewter, and I do." Nabby could hardly believe that Lonzo was actually talking to her about himself. "Indeed, I too wish you had not been apprenticed to Master Butler, for otherwise I might have had a chance."

Lonzo lowered his voice to a whisper. "If I knew I could get another place—" he began, but then he resumed his usual blustering talk. "A girl? Master Butler would never take a girl as apprentice."

"Better a girl than a boy who has no wish to learn," Nabby flared.

She wondered if any carpenters in Boston were in need of apprentices. If so, she would be tempted to try to persuade Master Butler to release Lonzo from his indenture. She would, that is, if she were sure Master Butler would take her in his stead.

"Lonzo," she began doubtfully, "mayhap we could—" but he left her and veered to the other side of the street as a column of soldiers, weary-faced and travel-worn, trudged by.

Nabby flattened herself against a wall to let them pass. This was doubtless the end of another exercise to keep the soldiers in trim. General Gage, so Nabby had heard, was forever sending his troops across the Neck on marches through the countryside, both to acquaint them with the terrain and to keep the rebels off balance. Such marches always caused a flurry of excitement and often the hasty mustering of militia on village greens. Officers who traveled the country roads to pick up any information they could were watched from every window and sometimes followed by hostile farmers, according to Will, whose master snatched news for his paper from every breeze that blew. The talk was that he did not print it all, lest some of it prove useful to the

British, determined to stamp out rebellion. As though her thoughts had conjured him up, Will plucked at her sleeve. He gestured toward the marching column.

"Back from a bootless errand, for once," he said gleefully. "The report is that the soldiery embarked by water to Charlestown again, this time to spike a battery of cannon before the provincials could hide them in somebody's barn for future need. To their surprise, the guns had vanished as though by magic."

"Vanished?" Nabby parroted. "As though by magic?"

Will grinned at her. "The magic of a pewter dram bottle," he said, "and a brown-and-white cow."

The dram bottle, the cow, and the hidden can-
non in Charlestown—to save her soul, Nabby could
not figure out the connection. She felt small and dim-
witted as Will grinned down at her. When had he
grown so much taller than she?

"Give me a hint," she begged, but he only laughed.

"You already have information aplenty. If your
wits are as sharp as I think they are, you will have the
answer soon enough."

Nabby scowled. "If I were a boy, you would tell
me. It is only girls who must obey and never know
why."

"Say you so?" Will's voice was indignant. "I must
do as I am bid, too, and learn what I can by looking
and listening. My master and his friends Dr. Warren,
Paul Revere, Sam and John Adams meet night after
night at the Green Dragon or the Long Room Club
over the print shop, planning ways to pass on information to the countryside in case the express riders should
not be able to get through sometime. This matter of
Charlestown was one such device."

"Which I could not betray," Nabby said tartly,

"since I cannot make head or tail of it. Tell me, then, what it was that the boy in the green boat brought for Master Butler."

"That is for Master Butler to tell if he wishes you to know. I have hinted at too much already in the matter."

"Will Truax," Nabby exploded, "you are quite the most irritating boy I have ever known! What harm could come from my knowing that?"

Will gave her a cool look. "None, in my opinion, but you and I are not in charge, clever though we may be. Some must be leaders and others followers in the rebel cause."

There were days when Nabby wished she had never heard of the rebel cause. As fall wore on into winter, she felt herself slipping steadily backward from her only true goal, which was to become a pewterer. Neither she nor Emily, who had finished her wriggled work, were ever asked into the workroom now. Master Butler himself seemed to accomplish little, although he worked with the door closed almost every night after Lonzo had hurried out for whatever pastime he and his fellows could find. The display of tankards and plates in the shop was scantier than ever, and few customers came in to look at what little there was.

"Who thinks on pewter in times like these?" Master Butler said gloomily one night. "If we can only struggle through the winter, Jeremiah Curtin will take what stock I have that is suitable to sell in the back country." His face turned bleak. "And then we must struggle through the summer until he returns since I doubt that he can pay me in advance after an idle winter himself."

In November, the British soldiers struck their tents on the Common and scattered into winter quarters all over town: warehouses, distilleries, sail lofts, Back Street near the pewterer who had shown Nabby the wriggled work, and any households unlucky enough to have room for them.

"Fortunately we have not an inch of spare space," Master Butler said. "It would wreak havoc were we to have a soldier in the house, especially now."

Especially now? That meant that something was brewing, although Nabby had no idea what it might be. Many of those loyal to the crown were moving from their homes in the open countryside into town, where they could be protected by the British army and the surrounding barriers of harbor and river that made Boston almost an island. The rebels continued to keep the town in an uproar and to pass the word to their friends outside about Gage's plans almost as soon as he made them. A flood of broadsides urged British soldiers to desert and flee to the country villages to help the rebels. Some of them did, walking out through the Neck disguised as countrymen going home from a visit. Others were persuaded to sell their "Brown Bess" muskets to the rebels and to claim they had been stolen, as indeed some of them had. These, with whatever firearms the Boston patriots could contribute, were sent to Concord and elsewhere to be ready for use if need be.

Nabby wondered how the guns could be smuggled

out except by boat on a moonless night. The cows, like the soldiers, were in winter quarters, and so there could be no more messages carried to the harbor islets and passed on to the countryside. Not only that, but any citizen of Boston who left town by way of the Neck, which was the only exit by land, must get a pass from a major at Province House, giving a good reason for going.

"Sick relatives, merchandise to be sold elsewhere, weddings, funerals—there are a dozen excuses for those who are not known troublemakers," Will said. "I have been back and forth a time or two myself of late, gone to visit my country cousins."

"Of whom I believe you have none," said Nabby. "Your tasks are a far cry from the usual chores of a printer's apprentice."

"Not so very far, everything considered. Besides, nothing is as usual nowadays."

Nabby learned the truth of that a few days later when a wagon drawn by a clumping farm horse stopped in front of Master Butler's. On the seat sat a country-man and his plump wife, well bundled against the chill. The man came hurriedly into the shop, which Nabby was tending while Mistress Butler tarried on Long Wharf for a gossip with the Widow Parsons.

"Pray tell Master Butler that Caleb Harmony is here from the countryside to deliver a load of provisions for the British army and would have a word with him at once. I am in the market for some items of his making."

Nabby, on the point of saying that Master Butler would not wish to speak with anyone who aided the occupying forces with provisions or anything else, bit back the words. The sale of even a pair of pewter plates, which, from the looks, would be all this man could afford, would ease the pressure on Master Butler's purse.

"We have fine tankards to show," Nabby said perversely, "and note the graceful curve of the handle on yonder teapot. My master spent many an hour perfecting that piece of work."

"Make haste, girl." Caleb Harmony was shuffling back and forth like a bear in a cage. "I have far to go, across the Neck and on past Menotomy before night catches me."

Night and the patriots, ever watchful for British sympathizers. Nabby tossed her head and went to fetch Master Butler.

"A man named Caleb Harmony," she said haughtily, "who has brought a wagonload of provisions for the British, wishes to buy pewter from you, but I think—"

"Think less," Master Butler snapped, "especially about things you know naught of. I am acquainted with the man, at least by name, and will deal with this matter as I deem best."

He hurried down the hall to the shop, where Caleb Harmony was waiting impatiently.

"You have finished my order?" he asked. "Candlesticks—"

"To light the way to freedom."

"And spoons—"

"To feed those hungry for liberty."

Nabby listened, openmouthed, to this curious exchange. Lacking good metal, Master Butler had made no candlesticks for some time and precious few spoons either, although mayhap he had been working on such an order during his nights in the workroom. Suddenly he seemed to remember that Nabby was there.

"On a crisp day like this, you and Emily should be out to take the air ere winter closes in for good." Nabby looked outside, where Caleb Harmony's wife was hunched against a blustery wind like a robin returned too early from warmer climes. "Wrap Emily well, with an extra shawl for her lap, and be off."

"Yes, sir." Nabby retreated sulkily to the kitchen and Emily. "We are to go out, on your father's orders."

Emily, ever happy to leave the house, no matter what the weather, struggled to her feet to put on her cloak and hobble to the wheeled chair. Just as Nabby was pushing her from kitchen to shop, Master Butler, red-faced, rose from behind the counter with two lumpy canvas sacks.

"Here you are," he told Caleb Harmony, "and I will fill more orders as the right metal comes to hand. Indeed, I—" He stopped in mid-sentence. "Two British soldiers are questioning your wife."

Caleb Harmony rushed to the window. "And soon will be questioning us, too, and, worse, searching the house as well."

"For spoons and candlesticks?" asked Nabby. "Since these items are so dangerous, why do Emily and I not take them with us to enjoy the bracing air as we did with the dram bottle?"

"Good girl!" Master Butler stuffed the canvas bags behind Emily's cushions. "Saunter forth as always—Emily, you have charcoal and paper?—and seize any chance to approach our friend Harmony after he leaves here. Then you must devise some way to transfer the sacks without anyone's seeing."

"If all else fails, I shall ask permission to make a sketch of the wagon," said Emily.

"I must depend on you," her father said, "on you and Nabby."

Nabby was struggling to open the heavy door just as the British soldiers were about to enter. One of them held it for her and even eased the wheeled chair over the threshold. Nabby gave him a dazzling smile.

"My thanks, sir. This vehicle is often clumsy to maneuver."

Pretending to tuck Emily in more warmly, she loitered long enough to hear Master Butler say, "May I serve you, sirs? I have only a small stock but of superior quality."

Nabby sniffed as they approached the farm wagon.

"From the smell, I judge the provisions have been exchanged for refuse from the British stables," she muttered into Emily's ear. Barely breaking stride, she nodded to Caleb Harmony's wife. "A chilly day and a long trip ahead, your husband tells us." The woman, seemingly frozen with fright, stared straight ahead. "Have no fear. The items you came for are safe, where the redcoats will never find them." She strolled calmly on with Emily. "Spoons and candlesticks! A likely story! I suppose your educated back cannot tell what is in those canvas bags?"

Emily wriggled against the cushions. "No more than I could tell what I leaned against on the day of the swimming cows," she said ruefully, "save that the bags are crammed full of small lumps like—"

"Like leaden shot, think you," Nabby cried in sudden inspiration, "for use in the muskets our militiamen keep ready?"

Emily snuggled deeper. "Mayhap. I have never leaned against any lead bullets before."

Nabby took care to turn into a street from which she could watch the wagon without seeming to do so.

"If Caleb Harmony brings provisions to the army and takes back stable refuse for his fields, he can go and come through the Neck without question," she said. "Still, 'tis a deal of trouble just for some ammunition. Surely the minutemen can make their own."

"The wagon is moving down Long Lane," said Emily, "and the soldiers, empty-handed, are seemingly bound for Fort Hill."

"Then we will go in quite another direction, mayhap catching up with the Harmonys at the Liberty Tree. Then we must find a way to pass them our cargo."

"How, Nabby?" asked Emily with sublime faith.

"I will think on it. We could pause for you to make a sketch, as you said, though that is apt to draw spectators, whom we do not need." Her thoughts churned dizzily. "Alas, we have little time to work out a plan."

"But my father is depending on us," said Emily.

Nabby eased the chair around a hole in the street.

"Did I not take care, I could break a wheel and send you careening into the street. We— Oh, there they are!" The wagon was coming slowly up Essex

Street to the grove of elms that included the ancient Liberty Tree, tallest of all. "Not many people are about, but even those are too many. However, the rich scent of the wagon's cargo may keep them at a distance."

Caleb Harmony had now stopped as though to rest his horse before he must turn onto Orange Street and leave Boston by way of the Neck. Nabby made desperate plans.

"Emily, when we come alongside the wagon, pray let your drawing materials slip out of your hands into the street, between the wagon and the wheel of your chair. I will tell you the exact moment. Also, brace yourself firmly against a lurch of the chair. A small accident is about to happen." Not even glancing at Caleb Harmony, Nabby pushed the chair beside the wagon as though to pass in the opposite direction. "Now!"

Emily dropped paper and charcoal. As Nabby bent as though to pick them up, she wrenched out the pin that held the wheel firm on the axle. Breaking a fingernail, she pried off the nut and let the wheel tilt sideways. Emily gave a convincing cry. Nabby looked up into Mistress Harmony's face as Caleb leaped down from the other side of the wagon and came to the rescue.

"The pin slipped out," said Nabby, as though to a stranger. "If you can find it for me— Fear not, Emily. The chair will not overturn. This kind man will fix it in no time. Here, let me rearrange your pillows."

As Caleb Harmony bent to inspect the wheel, his wife, who had not moved from her seat on the wagon, twitched a finger toward the straw that lay deep under

her feet to keep out the cold. Under cover of Caleb Harmony's broad back, Nabby slid the canvas bags out, unseen, from behind Emily's cushion and stowed them under the spread of the woman's full skirts.

"Here it is!" Nabby cried. "The pin that slipped out and the nut with it."

It took only a moment to put the wheel back in place. Caleb Harmony lumbered to his feet.

"All is well, girl," he said. "You may safely go on your way."

"I thank you with all my heart," she said, "and may you have a safe trip home."

"Were you not afraid?" Emily asked as Nabby pushed the chair back toward Milk Street.

"Nay," Nabby began, "I was— Oh, Emily, I was shaking with fright and still am. Suppose a British soldier should have seen me handing over the"—she lowered her voice—"candlesticks and spoons, and suppose that Caleb Harmony does not pass the Neck safely to the countryside."

Still, the British must know him well from his bringing provisions for them, and surely they would pay no heed to his portly wife, sitting so stolidly in the wagon with her skirts spread around her and her feet deep in the straw.

Master Butler was prowling from kitchen to shop when the girls came home.

"All went well?" he asked with more anxiety than he usually showed. "My usefulness would be at an end if Caleb Harmony were caught with the—"

"Indeed, sir," said Nabby, "if all the man can

smuggle out in a wagon are two bags of ammunition, it would hardly seem worth the trouble."

"There are other things buried beneath the stable refuse," Master Butler said.

"Muskets!" cried Nabby.

"You think so? Think away, for what you do not positively know will never hurt you. Now, tell me your tale."

He listened soberly. "You are clever girls, and brave ones, too," he said finally.

"Nabby is the clever one," Emily said, "and she has surely earned a reward. Father, will you not allow her to help with the pewtering sometimes?"

"She has indeed earned a reward," Master Butler said slowly, "and so have you, but I have barely enough work to keep Lonzo out of mischief. Besides, rewards, though deserved, should not be expected for serving the cause of liberty. We are all making sacrifices."

Always the same story—Nabby tried to swallow her disappointment, but she could not hold back a little barb that she hoped would sting Master Butler a bit.

"Pray, sir, what tale did you tell the British soldiers who were here when Emily and I left on the dangerous task that you sent two young girls to perform?"

Master Butler gave her a sharp look. "At your suggestion, may I remind you? As for the redcoats, I told them that I had an order from Caleb Harmony that was not yet complete because of a shortage of metal." Nabby lifted her eyebrows. "And that is the truth, for the minutemen, I doubt not, need all the ammunition I and others can provide. I also offered a tour of inspection, which the soldiers declined."

Nabby went soberly to bed that night to dream of riding with Caleb Harmony atop a load of straw concealing spoons, candlesticks, and pewter dram bottles marked CH. Just as a pair of British soldiers began probing through the straw with their bayonets, she awoke in a quiver to the sound of voices belowstairs. In the early-morning light she scrambled into her clothes and, as Emily watched wide-eyed from her bed, tiptoed to the head of the stairs to listen.

"Bring him in!" Master Butler was saying to someone just outside the street door. Lonzo, disheveled and wild of eye, stumbled in between two men of the watch. "The battle of the alepots, boy?" Lonzo held his head. Master Butler turned to the watch. "You found him lying in the street? My thanks for returning him, though 'tis no great favor." He gave Lonzo a shake, and the boy moaned. "Out all night in the grog shops, eh? For that, I could cancel your articles of apprenticeship. What say you to that?"

Over Master Butler's shoulder, Lonzo gave the fascinated Nabby a wink and a grin of satisfaction before he slid to the floor like a bag of meal.

12

"*Nabby!*" *Master Butler called, "Hasten below-*stairs! Lonzo is indisposed, and I have need of you!"

"Yes, sir, the moment Emily is dressed for the day." Nabby bent to whisper in Emily's ear. "Lonzo is no more drunk than I am, but whatever his reason for this pretense, it gives me a chance to return to the workroom."

She spent two blissful days there, holding the molds firmly together for the pouring of the metal and turning the great wheel for the burnishing, while Lonzo moped in his room.

"I will not starve the boy," said Master Butler. "Nabby, you may take him his meals if he is in any state to eat them. Certainly he has no head for strong drink, a fact that I trust he will remember in future."

Lonzo was as hungry as a starving wolf and as lively as a chipmunk except when Master Butler came to see how he did.

"Has he said aught about releasing me from my indenture?" Lonzo asked Nabby on the second day.

"Not to me." Nabby looked at him curiously. "How would you make your way if he set you adrift?"

"I had work with the British carpenters in the evenings," Lonzo mumbled, "and could get more, for they are desperate for help. Then it came to me that I might escape Master Butler's bondage once and for all by disgracing him in the streets."

"Good fortune to you," said Nabby, "though I fear Master Butler is as determined to make you into a pewterer as you are not to become one."

Lonzo emerged from his room at last, and Nabby, who had been helping Master Butler with a tulip tankard, was sent back to Emily, the kitchen, and an occasional stroll through Boston.

Although Master Butler said little, she gathered that Lonzo was making all manner of mistakes—holding the molds too loosely and once managing to drop a dollop of molten metal on a plate that was awaiting its final burnishing. Caleb Harmony did not return, and Master Butler no longer worked at night, doubtless for fear Lonzo, confined to the house for penance, might see what he was making.

"If you were to let him run free again at night," said Nabby, "you would be able to do your work for the rebels again, unless you have not been able to find the lead you need."

"I have lead," Master Butler said. "Some of our fishermen, who refuse to fish for the British and so are kept on dry land with the rest of us, have contributed their sinkers for the purpose." He sighed. "I still cannot find it in my heart to use my small store of pewter alloy to make bullets. Truth to tell, I had as lief not make bullets at all, but Massachusetts must not be helpless if it comes to out-and-out war."

"You think it will?"

"Sooner or later, but where and when I cannot say. If the complaints of the colonies are not remedied, as indeed they have not been yet, the Second Continental Congress will convene in Philadelphia next May to take more drastic action."

December, January, February—the winter dragged on into 1775, so unseasonably mild that the Charles River never froze over.

"Which is a relief to the British," said Will Truax, "for they feared that, once the river froze, our rural friends would swarm across the ice to liberate us."

As it was, everybody was miserably cooped up in town. The British soldiery mistrusted the citizens in general, a mistrust that was heartily returned. Those loyal to the crown feared the rebels, and the rebels despised the Loyalists.

"And so we all snap at one another like ill-tempered dogs," said Master Butler, who, having turned Lonzo loose at night again, now enlisted Nabby's help in casting more musket balls while Emily watched from her chair.

From its hiding place under the counter in the shop, he fetched the brass bullet mold, hinged at one end, with handles at the other, and a trench on either edge into which the lead was poured to fill twenty-four tiny cups, twelve to a side.

"So that is what I leaned against all the way home on the day of the swimming cows," said Emily. "My back remembers the shape of it much too well."

"But why all the secrecy for what must be a common-enough article?" Nabby asked.

"Amongst all my molds, naturally I had none for musket balls," said Master Butler, "so Caleb Harmony, on Jeremiah Curtin's advice, sent one of the right caliber for many of the minutemen's weapons. With the British snooping everywhere, there seemed no point in making a public presentation."

"Caleb Harmony again! Were those his initials you scratched on the bottom of the dram bottle?"

Master Butler ladled molten lead from the pot. "Hold the mold steady on its edge, Nabby!" He dripped the metal into one of the trenches, from which it ran down into the cups. "What a relief to have help! When I did this alone, I wished for three hands or even four. In a few moments when the lead in this set of cups has cooled enough, we will turn the mold over and fill the other trench." He set the ladle down on the workbench. "As for the dram bottle, it was an innocent-looking device for letting our sympathizers on the mainland know the destination of the British raiding party, plus the date and the mode of travel. *CH* stood only for Charlestown and had naught to do with Caleb Harmony." His voice turned impatient. "What does it matter now, except as a puzzle to amuse you and Emily? The episode is past, and events of much greater import loom on the horizon."

"Yes, sir." Nabby did not care to nurture the idea that she and Emily were merely silly girls with no interest in the fate of the colonies. "I will turn my thoughts to other matters."

She turned them back again that night when she and Emily were lying in their beds.

"*CH* for Charlestown," she murmured to Emily,

"but your father mentioned also the date and the way the soldiers traveled. September 8, I think?"

"Ninth month, eighth day," Emily said airily, "and that takes care of the '9' and the '8.' Am I not clever?"

"Indeed." Nabby was crestfallen. "We have it from your father's own lips that we are both clever, though in this matter I lag far behind."

"We must all lag behind sometimes, in one way or another." Emily, who seldom referred to her lameness, sounded cheerful enough. "As for the route, the soldiers went by boat, did they not?" She paused. "Nabby, is there water in the mug on the table? I have a tickle in my throat."

Nabby leaped out of bed in the darkness and held the mug to Emily's lips. "Water!" she exclaimed. "They went by water, and there was water in that dram bottle."

Emily spluttered. "Do not drown me in water! for all that, I think you have solved the rest of the riddle, so we are even now."

Nabby doubted it. Emily's demand for water had been too neatly timed to be merely accidental.

"How fortunate for the patriots' cause that I did not try to devise that cipher I spoke of," Nabby said ruefully, "since I cannot work out anybody else's message without help."

The next night, Master Butler, with some reluctance, allowed Emily to hold the bullet mold while Nabby poured the molten metal.

"You have a steady hand," he told Nabby.

"From ladling broth and stew."

She looked scornfully at the heap of musket balls. She would so much rather work with real pewter and turn out satiny tankards and teapots. Still, she reminded herself that, tiresome though the product was, she was being permitted to pour the metal at last—another small step forward.

On a blustery March day, the Widow Parsons beckoned Nabby into her tobacco shop to give her two ingots of tin that had been passed from hand to hand all the way from Salem and Silas Bridges.

"Along with a length of cherry ribbon for me," the widow said.

"How will Master Butler send Silas the money," asked Nabby, "if indeed he has any to send?"

The Widow Parsons brought out a grimy note that looked as though it had been folded and unfolded a hundred times.

"If I read this aright, Master Butler is not to pay until the *Boston Traveller* returns yet again, for she weighed anchor for England the moment her cargo was unloaded and another put aboard."

Nabby looked longingly at the tin. She hesitated to remind Master Butler that he had promised to repair her porringer with the next good alloy. Since Jeremiah Curtin, preparing to start on his spring trip, had almost stripped the shop of pewter, Master Butler would need to use every bit of metal he could get to replenish his shelves. As predicted, the peddler had been able to pay for only a small part of the pewter, with the balance due when he returned in the fall.

"Do you not fear to set foot in the streets," the widow asked, "after last night's uproar?"

Nabby laughed. "Not I! Indeed I wish I had been there to see."

What had begun as an observance of the fifth anniversary of the Boston Massacre, had ended absurdly just when it seemed that a clash between the British and the patriots was inevitable. British officers had filed into the Old South Meeting House, ready, so Will Truax said, to seize the rebel leaders if the speech-making grew too violent. There was considerable heckling, and at one point a British redcoat shouted, "Fie! Fie!"—which sounded so much like "Fire! Fire!" that the audience departed hastily through doors and windows like mice fleeing the cat.

"An exciting night, indeed," Will Truax had said, "but at least none of our true patriots were seized."

All the same, in the early spring many of the top rebel leaders—Dr. Warren excepted—thought it best to leave Boston and disappear into the countryside lest they be arrested and so become useless to the patriot cause. Nabby, Emily, and Master Butler continued to make musket balls and to dispatch them to Concord by Caleb Harmony, who was still able to come and go as he pleased with his stores of provisions and his return cargo from the stables.

"A fat British colonel and a thin private have been spying out the country Worcester and Concord way under guise of day laborers looking for work," he reported. "Oh, what a masquerade! Despite their leathern breeches and coarse neckerchiefs, a girl serving in a tavern recognized one of them since she had been employed in Boston not long since. The colonel hastened back to town, but the young private pressed on and no doubt reported back to General Gage our many stores in both towns."

Master Butler no longer shooed Nabby and Emily away during this passing on of news.

"They have earned our trust," he told Caleb Harmony, who nodded.

Nabby sighed. They had earned just enough trust to listen to what was going on but not enough to be allowed to do more in the workroom than to help make the endless lead shot. The making of pewter seemed to require trust of another kind, she thought wearily: trust that she could work as well as any boy, trust in her ability to learn, trust in her fondness for the craft. Surely all these points were as clear as daylight to anyone but Master Butler, who seemed determined not to believe.

Since all else was failing her, Nabby took to carrying her poor flawed porringer in her pocket again, where she could touch it for luck as she and Emily took their daily walks. Usually they ended up on Long Wharf, from which they had a good view of the British ships riding at anchor, watchdogs of the harbor.

"They have put their longboats into the water astern of the warships," Nabby said in surprise one raw April Saturday. She watched the boats bobbing on the whitecaps. "Now what is the meaning of that?"

By Tuesday the eighteenth, it was plain that something was afoot. Will Truax, hurrying to report to the printer, told Master Butler that a talkative groom in the British stables had said that several young officers were having their horses shod as though for a special expedition. A few minutes later a neighbor slipped in with the news that a grenadier billeted at her house had had a message to report to the Common at ten that night with full equipment.

"Nabby, pray follow Will Truax," Master Butler said, "and give him the news of the grenadiers. He will see that it reaches the right people."

"Yes, sir. And may I go then to the Widow Parsons for whatever news she may have?"

"Go where you will." His mind seemed elsewhere. "I have duties myself."

He clapped his hat on his head and hurried to the door.

"Your supper, Tobias!" Mistress Butler cried.

"Feed it to Lonzo, for I may not be home before cockcrow."

He was out of sight by the time Nabby had put on her cloak. She caught Will on Hanover Street, not far from Dr. Warren's house, which had become information headquarters for the rebels.

"I cannot stop a moment," said Will when he had heard Nabby's news. "Just in the last few minutes, I learned that the young officers I spoke of have already ridden across the Neck with much talk of dinner in the country, three senior officers have been closeted with General Gage this long time, and there is a great collecting of gear among the light infantry and grenadiers." He hurried on so fast that Nabby could hardly keep up. "Pray go home, for it is growing dark and I would not wish harm to befall you."

"Nor I you," said Nabby.

She frowned. For all his being a tall, husky boy, harm was much more likely to befall him than it was her, for the Marines billeted not far away in North Square would not hesitate to stop any man or boy they suspected of mischief. Nabby moved back into the shadows and watched Will as he darted into the back door of Dr. Warren's house. She reached into her pocket and clutched the porringer for comfort. She was shivering, half from fright and half from a chilly wind, but she had no intention of going home. Had not Master Butler given her permission to go where she wished?

She slipped still deeper into shadow as a few soldiers with their gear walked silently past in the direction of the Common. Nabby was tempted to follow to see whether the troops would march out through the Neck or embark by water on the Charles River. She leaned to the latter, remembering the longboats flocking astern of the warships like chicks around the mother hen.

Dark figures, glimpsed only briefly as Dr. Warren's back door opened a crack and quickly closed again, kept coming and going. Nabby, usually as brave as a lion anywhere in Boston, felt a quiver of panic. It was so dark—no moon yet and only a few stars peering now and then through patchy clouds. The glow from the famous streetlamps, if indeed any were lighted tonight, did not penetrate to Nabby's hiding place behind a huge bush. Where was Will? Mayhap he had left Dr. Warren's by another door and was at the other end of Boston by now. Nabby was creeping from behind the bush when something moved in the darkness behind her. She had time only to utter a squeak before a hand was clapped over her mouth and a strong arm jerked her back into hiding.

"The sentries!" a voice hissed in her ear as booted feet passed with measured tread. Nabby stood frozen as her captor held her as helpless as a rabbit in a snare. "Have we not problems enough without a curious girl drawing the attention of the British?"

"Will!" Torn between anger and relief, Nabby pulled his fingers away from her mouth and turned to face him. "I was only waiting for you to come out."

"Tell me later," Will said brusquely. "Since you did not heed my advice to go home, I must now take you with me while I run an urgent errand, which cannot be delayed a moment. Come along! No, not that way. Over the wall and down the lane, and do not utter a word."

They ran down back ways, veering well around North Square when they saw redcoats lined up as though about to march. They dodged through narrow lanes and private yards and even among the ghostly stones of a burying ground and came at last to a little wharf tucked almost out of sight at the edge of the water. Will knelt on the low wharf to sight along the shoreline.

"We are in time," he said. "The boat is still here."

"It is? I can see nothing," said Nabby, breathless from their flight through the town. "You plan to go to sea again?"

"Not I! I am sent merely to watch and make sure that Paul Revere and his two oarsmen get safely away."

"Away where?" asked Nabby.

"Across the Charlestown ferryway, and then he will ride to Lexington to warn Sam Adams and John Hancock that the British are on the march and doubtless eager to lay hands on them. William Dawes, who can clown his way over the Neck at will with quips and gifts of strong drink, has already been dispatched by land, to make sure that at least one man gets through. One or both will then carry the message on to Concord, for so large a body of troops must surely have a more urgent mission than capturing two men, important though they be to the cause."

"They will be looking for the stores of supplies and ammunition stored at Concord, some of it of our making." Nabby glanced out to the ferryway, where the riding lights of the *Somerset* bobbed up and down above the dark water. "How will Master Revere pass unnoticed almost under the stern of the man-of-war?"

"How indeed? Muffled oars and a moon hidden by clouds at the right moment would help, as well as the prayers of the friends of liberty."

Nabby looked back toward the North Church, whose spire, faintly silhouetted now against the light of a rising moon, was the tallest in Boston.

"I think I saw a flare of light in the steeple," she said, "as though someone had lighted a pair of lanterns."

She strained to see more clearly, but the spire was dark again.

"Two lanterns?" Will asked. "That will tell the patriots on the opposite shore that the troops are moving by water." He turned back to stare out over the Charles. "Far to the left of the *Somerset,* can you see darker shadows that could be longboats heading for Lechmere's Point, or is that but a figment of the mind?"

"If I were a cat that could see in the dark, I would know more of what is happening," said Nabby, "but there may be boats there, filled, no doubt, with red-coats by the hundreds. Oh, where is Master Revere? He must hasten to beat the troops to Lexington."

"A good horse will be saddled and ready for him on the far shore," said Will, "while the redcoats must slog along afoot through marshy land. Besides, think of all the things that can go wrong for the British. Some of the boats may have to go back for a second load, someone may have mixed up the orders, or—" He pulled her away from the wharf. "Take cover. Some-one is coming."

A bulky man—Paul Revere, surely—and his two oarsmen slipped silently to the edge of the water and settled themselves in the almost invisible boat with only a faint ripple of the water. A pause, mayhap to muffle the oars, and the boat moved out into the ferry-way.

"He must go well to seaward, which makes the crossing that much longer." Will's voice was a mere whisper of sound.

"And the moon is well up the sky," Nabby said in despair. "Will, let us draw away from the shore, lest—"

"Are you afraid?" Will was watching the cautious progress of the boat.

"Nay, I am not, but if the British patrol should find us here, they would wonder why and might start gazing out over the water themselves. A loud halloo would rouse the *Somerset* and— Oh, Will, do hurry!"

Her fears were justified, for she and Will had barely left the wharf and turned onto the nearest street before two redcoats with a lantern barred their way.

"Halt, there! Stand and state your business!"

"My business is my own!" Will said defiantly, but Nabby darted past the soldiers so that they must turn their backs on the waterfront to capture her again.

"Not so fast, my girl!" One of the redcoats jerked his head toward Will, who was now standing protectively beside Nabby. "You, boy, raise your hands over your head and be quick about it." He turned to his companion. "Search him for messages. Methinks I saw that head of red hair near Dr. Warren's house earlier tonight."

"Cannot a man walk through the streets in peace?" Will said in an innocent voice. "But search away. I am only a humble apprentice, with neither messages nor weapons."

Nabby stood as though terrified, but she was calculating how much time Master Revere would need to reach the far shore. When the redcoats saw that Will had nothing of import with him, they would let him go and might then proceed toward the ferryway, possibly soon enough to spy the rowboat. That must not happen, but how could she prevent it? She reached into her pocket to make sure her lucky porringer was safe—if indeed it *was* lucky.

"What have you there, girl?" one of the soldiers demanded. "She-rebels are as dangerous as their men. Out with it!"

"I will not!" Nabby shook with anger. If once he laid hands on the porringer, he would pocket it himself or take it away to see whether anyone could read

a message from the touchmark. In either case, it would be gone forever. "Never will I give it up! Never!"

"Say you so?" the redcoat blustered. "We'll see about that!"

Nabby peered desperately past the small pool of light made by the lantern. A buzz of voices told her that a party of townspeople was approaching, mayhap from watching the soldiers embark from the Common. With luck, she might manage to keep the redcoats' attention from Paul Revere and the waterfront and save her porringer at the same time. With a blood-curdling shriek, she kicked over the lantern and flung the porringer toward the depths of the nearest bush. Her aim failed as the redcoat caught her arm, and the porringer landed with a clang on the cobblestones and bounced away into the darkness.

"Let me go!" Nabby screamed at the top of her lungs. She writhed out of the grasp of her captor. "Thieves! Robbers! Help me, good people! Help!"

"I could find my porringer." Nabby prowled miserably from window to window. "I *know* I could, if only—"

If only Master Butler would let her out of the house, where she had been cooped up all day long on his stern orders. The sun was setting—nearly a whole day gone with no news, at least in this house, either of Paul Revere's crossing or of the lost porringer.

"If I were able, I would go hunting for it myself." Emily put her hand comfortingly into Nabby's.

"I am sure you would." Nabby turned as the kitchen door eased open and Master Butler slipped in with a cautious glance behind him. "You have news, sir? Did Paul Revere—"

"News indeed." Master Butler sank onto the bench beside the table. "I scarce know where to begin. First of all, Paul Revere was stopped—"

"Before he could reach the Charlestown shore?" Horrified, Nabby stared at him. "Then the watch on the *Somerset* must have spied him, for I know those two redcoats did not note his boat from the Boston side of the water."

"Nor did anybody else in the whole North End, from what I hear. With the hullabaloo you put up, Revere could have sailed past the *Somerset* with fifers and drummers and nobody on shore would have heard or seen any of it." For all his chaffing words, Master Butler's voice was tight with strain. "It appears that you are a heroine, at least if good intentions count."

Nabby shook her head. She had no wish to be thought a heroine but only to have her porringer back. Truth to tell, the evening before was rather blurred in her mind—doors flying open all up and down the street at her screams, angry citizens rushing to her rescue, faces appearing and disappearing out of the darkness, among them Lonzo's for a brief moment. But no, she could not be sure of that, any more than she could remember quite how she had escaped—a hand pulling her away from the center of the fracas, a push to the safety of the shadows. Then she and Will were running down the back streets, while behind them the night echoed with the uproar for which North Enders had long been famous.

"So Master Revere was captured, after all," she said dully.

"Our messengers bring word that he was not stopped until he had reached shore safely, mounted his waiting steed, and spread the alarm all the way to Lexington," Master Butler said. "There he warned Sam Adams and John Hancock to flee to safety. William Dawes, who had ridden overland by way of the Neck, joined him, but the two of them were halted by British officers on patrol, leaving Dr. Samuel Prescott of Concord, who had been visiting a girl in Lexington, to carry the word the rest of the way."

"And then? The stores were saved?"

"The redcoats paid a high price for what they managed to find—a quantity of musket balls and some barrels of flour that they threw into the Concord mill-pond." His face was grim. "Men were killed today, both British and colonials. Even now the redcoats, who got the worst of the battle, are being brought back to Boston with their wounded. They are thankful, I daresay, to be out of reach of our brave minutemen, who harried them all the way to Charlestown after the fighting at Lexington and Concord Bridge."

Mistress Butler gave a little cry. "Oh, Tobias! What will become of us now?"

"Why, nothing, God willing." Master Butler kept his voice calm, but Nabby read his anxiety in his face. "If I were General Gage, now that the shooting has begun, I would start arresting whatever rebel leaders I could lay my hands on—few enough now. Dr. Warren, I hear, slipped out today, leaving his patients in charge of another. Master Edes, I think, will take his press and go too, if he has not done so already. Boston will be kept more tightly guarded against the besieging colonials than ever before, but we can still be useful to the cause if we are discreet. After all, our past activities are not widely known."

"As you say." Mistress Butler, reassured, bustled to her work. "Nabby, ladle the stew. We need not starve because of all this." She turned to her husband. "You have found Lonzo?"

"I have not!" Master Butler snapped.

"But I—" Nabby began. "Has he run away?"

"So it seems. He has not been seen since last night, and his room is stripped of his few possessions. Good riddance, no doubt, but my failure with him is no feather in my cap."

"Where would he go?" Nabby wondered, although she thought she knew.

At this moment he was probably in one of the barracks aiding the carpenters who had been brought in from Nova Scotia. If he were wise, he would keep well under cover and ask to be shipped back north with the rest when his work was done. Master Butler, apparently with his mind on matters other than Lonzo, dipped his cornbread into the codfish stew.

"I have a good mold for dram bottles," he mused. "Should the other colonies join us in our battle against the British, there will be a true army, and every man in it must have a pewter dram bottle for his daily ration of spirits." He started as three faint taps came on the kitchen door. "I will go." He opened the door only a little to let Will Truax in his floppy countryman's hat come in from the darkness. "Just in time to sup." He made a place beside him. "I feared for your safety. Food for this brave lad, Nabby."

Will set a large basket on the floor beside him and pulled off his hat. Nabby stared.

"I have heard of hair turning white in a single night," she said, "but never from red to black."

"The best grade of printer's ink," said Will around a large mouthful of stew. "The British, when they have time to think of aught save their dead and wounded, may be interested in finding a red-haired apprentice." He managed a wan grin. "And a tall girl with a loud voice, though the British do not war on women and children, I hear." He turned serious. "Nabby, I have searched for your porringer through half the bushes in the North End today, but it is nowhere to be found."

"A foolhardy venture, under the circumstances," Master Butler grumbled. "Has your master no regard for your safety?"

"Too much, sir. He is sending me to his cousin in Watertown tonight"—he laid down his spoon—"on the Charlestown ferry, which is again unguarded. Since he is watched himself, he begs you to see me safely away, though I have no fear save of the rocking ferry."

"Tonight?" Nabby cried. "Oh, Will!"

What would life be like without Will, companion for her and Emily, purveyor of news and drawing paper? To her surprise, tears sprang to her eyes. She blinked them away, but not before Will had seen.

"Pray do not think my going is the end of the world," he said. "You will see me again soon enough."

"The end of the world? Do you deem yourself so important that I shall die without you?"

He grinned. "That's my Nabby, ever ready with a kind word. Well, then, think of me sometimes until we meet again."

"That I will!" she promised. "And forgive my sharp tongue. It conceals an anxious heart."

Master Butler arose. "We had best be on our way to the ferry," he said gruffly, "if you two are done with your billing and cooing."

Billing and cooing! If Master Butler thought there

was anything between her and Will, he would never teach her to make pewter, lest she leave him midway. Still, Will was a true friend, who had ventured forth at great risk today to search for her porringer—a deed that earned her affection.

"You are sure there is no danger?" Mistress Butler said as her husband and Will, with his basket on his arm, made ready to leave.

"A man thought to be accompanying his visiting son to the ferry"—Master Butler's voice was not quite steady—"will hardly be molested tonight. Nevertheless, blow out the candles so we may step through the doorway unnoticed."

Abovestairs with Emily after Master Butler had at last returned to say that Will was safely on his way, Nabby turned her eyes resolutely away from the table by the window, where the porringer had always shone in moonlight and sunlight. Since Will had searched in vain for it, she must accept the fact that she would never see it again. Someone would have picked it up— a redcoat last night or a passerby this morning.

Flinging the porringer away into the darkness had been the right strategy at the time, but "right" had a bitter taste to it now. She must, she feared, regard the porringer as her gift to the rebel cause, for had not Master Butler said that everyone was making sacrifices?

"But I am a grudging giver," Nabby muttered to the unheeding Emily, fast asleep after the fears of the evening.

Nabby lay long awake, remembering the day her father had pulled the porringer out of his seaman's pack in the tiny shop on Long Wharf.

"Nay, 'tis not to be sold in the shop," he had told her mother. "Nabby is to have it as a gift—of which she has had few enough."

In her memory the porringer was as perfect as though Lonzo had never dropped it into the melting pot and its sheen as bright as though it were still sitting on the table in the moonlight. With that, having no choice, she must be content.

She slept then and awoke late, to help Mistress Butler carry Emily downstairs, with never a word about Nabby's tardiness.

"Tobias is already in his workroom," she said as a still-sleepy Nabby ladled bowls of mush for herself and Emily. She had taken barely three spoonfuls before Master Butler's voice echoed through the house.

"Nabby! Nabby! I would have a word with you!"

What now? Surely she had done nothing he could complain about during the last day, shut up in the house as she had been, but mayhap he was harking back to past sins. She scurried fearfully into the workroom.

"The fire not mended, the floor not swept!" he roared. "How can you take Lonzo's place as my apprentice if you are remiss in your duties?"

Nabby stared, thunderstruck. "Oh, sir, do you truly mean it? I am to be your apprentice as I have wished for so long?"

"With Lonzo gone, I have no choice but to take a girl and hope for the best." His words were gruff, but there was a twinkle in his eyes for once. "You will do well, or I will know the reason why!"

"Oh, thank you, sir. First, shall I bring charcoal

to start the forge fire burning while I sweep the floor and tidy the tool shelves?"

"And then you may fetch Emily, for I shall need her, too, for wriggled work and other chores."

"Oh, sir!"

Breathless with joy, Nabby flew into the shed for the charcoal. What had seemed like one of the darkest times of her life was now shot with sunshine. She glanced into Lonzo's tiny room, empty save for pallet, chair, and table. A slip of tattered paper thrust between window frame and sash caught her eye. She pulled it through to the inside and read the straggling letters: "Yure porinjer is in the krook of the tree. Godbye. Lonzo."

"My porringer! My porringer!"

Forgetting Master Butler, charcoal, and apprenticeships, Nabby flew down the hall and out the kitchen door. A ray of light caught the sheen of the porringer, wedged into place where the lowest limb of the tree branched off. Her treasure was even more battered than before, but to her it was the most beautiful piece of pewter in Boston. She darted back to the workroom and held it out to Master Butler.

"Lonzo, of all people, rescued it for me," she said, between tears and laughter, "and left it in the tree."

She could picture him retrieving the porringer during the commotion in the North End and creeping back to hide it and leave his laboriously written note before he left Milk Street forever. Master Butler inspected the porringer.

"If you will bring the charcoal—twice is too often to tell even a new apprentice, but you may be excused